Crossing the Pa-Rak River

A Novel

by

Philip Kim

© Copyright 2006 Philip Kim

Cover Design by Author, Philip Kim
www.kimphilip.com
philipkim@kimphilip.com

All rights reserved. No part of this publication may be reproduced, stored in a retrieval system, or transmitted, in any form or by any means, electronic, mechanical, photocopying, recording, or otherwise, without the written prior permission of the author.

Note for Librarians: A cataloguing record for this book is available from Library and Archives Canada at www.collectionscanada.ca/amicus/index-e.html
ISBN 1-4251-0021-X

Offices in Canada, USA, Ireland and UK

Book sales for North America and international:
Trafford Publishing, 6E–2333 Government St.,
Victoria, BC V8T 4P4 CANADA
phone 250 383 6864 (toll-free 1 888 232 4444)
fax 250 383 6804; email to orders@trafford.com
Book sales in Europe:
Trafford Publishing (UK) Limited, 9 Park End Street, 2nd Floor
Oxford, UK OX1 1HH UNITED KINGDOM
phone +44 (0)1865 722 113 (local rate 0845 230 9601)
facsimile +44 (0)1865 722 868; info.uk@trafford.com
Order online at:
trafford.com/06-1778

10 9 8 7 6 5 4 3 2

This book is dedicated to my Father,
Sang Hoon Kim,
A spiritual mentor I admire

Acknowledgements

Thanks to my sons, Kwan Woo and Timothy Hyeunwoo, and my daughter in law Rochon Wan Hsien, who read the work. I would especially like to thank Young Ae, my wife, who supported me with just the right mixture of patience and encouragement. I would also like to offer my deep gratitude to my dear mother, Yong Hee Choi.

Author's Note

This is a true story, although it is intermingled with some fiction. As an eyewitness in the divided time of Korea, I felt compelled to write my personal experiences. I have a deep sympathy with the people who had been sacrificed as a result of the Korean War and who suffered from separation by the tragic division, and so have attempted to evoke the general effect of that division.

Table of Contents

The Final Haven

Last night's snowstorm had clothed the yellowish grass of Norbeck Memorial Park in a dazzling white shroud. An unsettling wind was dancing around the coffin like a ballerina without a purpose. At the conclusion of the pastor's brief benediction, the coffin was quickly lifted by a small crane and then flung down ruthlessly into the eternal abyss of time. I tossed a yellow chrysanthemum into the pit, and it gently caressed the top of my father's coffin. Mourners hurriedly filled the hole with wet soil, quickly erasing any trace of my father's existence. Soon after, the gathering began to disperse, one by one. All of a sudden, a sense of bereavement began to prick the core of my heart. Close to my father's new home stood a cherry tree, skeletal now, cloaked in its wintry white shroud. It stood in seeming indifference to my pain and to my destiny. Above, a wedged squadron of wild geese flew into the western sky, letting go a distant scream. A soothing voice reached my ears: "Do not worry son, at last I have found my final haven. There is no more need to escape, no more sorrow. Death is not a tragedy but, rather, it is bliss." I was then comforted by a sense of peaceful closure.

Crossing the Pa-Rak River

My father's sudden death drove my thoughts back to a particular day in early March of 1948. The skies were dark and dreary that day and the area where the Pa-Rak River and the Yellow Sea joined fused in a seamless, cohesive manner. Despite the threatening spirit that seemed to hover over the swirling waters, many would-be escapees fretfully waited for the lowest ebb of the tide, as if expecting a cleft through the waves, as Moses had provided at the Red Sea, hoping to wade to the south. Just before the break of day, at the darkest moments when the distinction between the sky and waters could not be made, fugitives stealthily slid into the cold water, committing their flesh and souls to the providence of God.

I was six years old when I crossed the 38th parallel. Mother carried me on her slender shoulders, letting my two legs swing free as if I were riding on the back of a horse. People around us were hushed, so as not to be detected by the Red Army scouts who were patrolling the military demarcation line. From time to time, vague figures were silhouetted like fleeting malevolent apparitions against the dark water. As the refugees groped their way across the river, searching for footholds on the shallow beckoning shore, the tide suddenly began to rise. Later, it was said that some among us who were carrying young babies on their backs had stuffed wads of cloth into the babies' small mouths in an effort to keep the babies silent. In the process of attempting to make the journey safe for all, they had sadly and inadvertently caused the suffocation of their own silenced children.

Yet, at daybreak, many families including ours had still not reached the safety of the shore. We were stuck in the middle of the river, at the mercy of the strong current which started to creep up to our chests. As if mocking the hopes of the wretched escapees, teasing them, the wild waves of the 38th parallel water churned around them, while their desperate dreams of freedom to the south seemed to burst along with the bubbles of the water's foam.

"Comrades! Comrades, come here!" Communist soldiers called out to us, waving their hands and fixing a long narrow wooden plank obliquely into the heart of the water against the bulwark. All the captured souls were locked in a temporary prison. Adults were shaking like drenched, furless cats.

"Hi, kid! Where is your father" the Communist interrogator asked me with a gentle face.

"He is dead," I answered instantly to his insistent query. He appeared to accept this as an unsophisticated reply from an innocent child. My mother had anticipated this type of situation and had prepared me in the event of its happening. Thus she had repeatedly told me: "In case somebody asks where your father is, just say that he is dead." Because this idea had been drilled into my head, I was able to deceive my interrogator as my mother had planned. The interrogator did not question me anymore.

I later heard that many men who had been captured were drafted into the People's Red Army after being tortured in cages for varying periods of time. The women and children were soon released. The Red examiner was relatively lenient to children and women. Changing his attitude, the investigator scolded my mother in a subdued voice. "Why are you fleeing to the south? I think you are stupid. You know, sooner or later, our Democratic People's Republic of Korea will achieve an earthly paradise. You have got to know that your attempt to escape from this great northern part of Korea is a betrayal of our fatherland and qualifies as an act against the people's ideology. Keep in mind: if you try to escape again, we are not going to forgive you next time." It was obvious that Mother was going to give birth soon. The interrogator released her in no time.

Soon after her release, while she was still drifting about aimlessly in the early dawn, she happened to encounter her remote relative, Mrs. Young Ju. Mother and Mrs. Young Ju's meeting was a stroke of luck on many levels; as the sun was rising, so was Mother's discomfort due to the impending birth. As fate would have it, Mrs. Young Ju was secretly waiting for a chance to escape to the south. "You look pale," she said. "Let's go to my retreat, and I will help you during your baby's delivery, ok?" Mother gladly agreed and, after a few days' stay at Mrs. Young Ju's temporary hut, my second younger brother came into the world of the divided time. On the day when the new baby saw the light first, both the child and the biting Siberian wind cried bitterly all day long.

In the meantime, a rumor was rampant that the 38th parallel would be enforced more tightly than ever. "We need to hurry before the line is sealed for good," said Mrs. Young Ju, "and no failing this time. We must succeed in crossing the line of fate.

But do not worry. I have already hired a good guide." She urged Mother to take another chance for her family's freedom. Almost totally exhausted from the suffering of parturition and the draining influence of malnutrition, Mother lapsed occasionally into short hallucinatory spells. These often took her back to dreams of the pleasant days when she had enjoyed a blissful life in her hometown, Sineui-Ju City, in the northernmost part of Korea, bordering on Manchuria in China.

After Mother arose from a short dream-filled sleep, Mrs. Young Ju advised her, "You had better wrap your legs tightly so that the swelling that often occurs after childbirth will not impede you and cause pain during your escape through cold waters." Even so, all feared that, after having given birth, the trauma of the cold water would be detrimental to Mother's health. When nighttime fell, it was pitch black due to the absent moon. We followed very closely after the guide. Hand in hand, we cut through the tough current whose waters were both the barrier between life and death, and between the north and freedom in the south. In the distant sky, little stars flickered like fireflies, as though they were alternately beckoning and taunting us. Mother murmured an incantation, praying for God's mercy in the dark waters where the ghost of God was drifting.

The guide was leading us calmly without making a single noise. Every snap of a twig or rustling of a branch created an eerie sense of paranoia as we plowed through the stream. When we finally reached the shore of the southern bank, the sky was tinted with the thin rose flush of impending dawn. As we had feared, mother's legs had become swollen. Her whole body was shaking like an aspen leaf. She stammered in confusion: "Where is my husband now?" Father was at that time employed as an engineer at the Hae-Ju chemical factory, located in Hae-Ju City, not too far north of the 38th parallel. Under strict surveillance by the Communist party, Hae-Ju was, essentially, a prison with no bars.

Two Opposite Roads

Trapped in Hae-Ju under the frantic red sky, full of blood stench and oppression, Father waited for any small chance to escape toward the south. The north Communist regime needed as many of the intelligentsia as it could hold onto in order to keep the infrastructure operating while it established total control. Even though he had been born a member of the bourgeoisie, the Communists treated him warmly, providing him with an official residence and good pay. Nevertheless, they were keeping him under tight scrutiny and close guard because he was the son of a wealthy farmer who had been classified as a member of the reactionary element. Father was nothing but a pitiable fish struggling to get free from the net.

In the deepest darkness of night, just before dawn, while he was sound asleep, my father was frequented by an unwanted visitor who was working at the same factory. The front gate would protest the loud knock. "Bang! Bang!" The visitor would call, "Comrade Kim! Comrade Kim!" The night man would keep pounding on the front gate until father was awakened and identified by the Communist secret partisan.

"What's the matter with you, bothering me this late at

night?" If father flared up at the rude intruder, the cell partisan would talk incessantly and insist that he was innocent of any foul intent. As the time went by, the uninvited guest made ever more frequent and belligerent visits. "Damned dog! This is torture!" my father would mutter. Each night the intimidating man appeared, father would be kept sitting up until dawn. Day and night, father felt constricted by invisible observers and distresses by the all-too-visible night specter's appearances.

One day, a group of senior members of the Communist party from the capital city, Pyeung-Yang, swarmed into the Hae-Ju chemical plant, without advance notice, for a strict inspection. The chief in charge of the factory and his top members made a fuss about their arrival and quickly prepared special entertainment and food for the inspectors. But shortly after they were served the best the plant had to offer, the chief from the Central Labor Party in Pyeung-Yang suddenly took a serious turn, scowling at all of those who worked in the factory. With his face distorted and twisted and his right fist pounding on the desk, he shouted in a coarse voice, "Comrades! Comrades, you are rotten! Where did you get all this good food? Do you understand what I am talking about?

He proceeded to launch into a prolonged tirade, reproaching the factory workers who had given him a cordial reception. He tediously preached Communist dogmas. He proclaimed, "Comrades! I am going to report your anti-revolutionary and Anti-Party activities to the Central Party! We have got to cleanse these spoiled elements of the great proletarian revolution for good." Those lower in factory hierarchy were reduced to hanging their heads in fear as they contemplated the possibility of a fateful purge in their future.

"Nonsense! He is blowing a lot of hot air. Do not take him

seriously!" Father snorted in mind because he knew Young Sup, the chief investigator who was threatening them, as a former classmate with whom he had studied at Kyeung-Sung University in Seoul City, before the liberation from the Japanese control over the Korean peninsula. Young Sup, however, pretended not to know his bosom friend, in order not to lose dignity in the face of his inferiors. Since their graduation from the university in March 1942, they had not heard news about each other. In their school days, they were sworn friends. Young Sup would enjoy much talk about Nietzsche, Karl Marx, and Dostoyevsky. He particularly worshipped Nietzsche with great passion. While clenching his fist in rage, Young Sup would passionately exclaim, "Nietzsche's word is right! God is dead! If God existed, how could He let our fatherland be cast away into the hands of the brutal invaders!"

In the early hours of the next morning, an unexpected thing happened. Enveloped in the shadows, the chief inspector, Young Sup, popped into his old friend's residence as silently as a ghost. They exchanged greetings. "Hey, Hoon!" "Hi! Young Sup!" They stood for a while, gazing at each other as tears glistened in the corners of their eyes. For the moment, Young Sup was no longer the rough fellow who had yelled so fervently. Then, in an instant, both men became friends again as in the past. "Hey, Hoon! It's been a really long time since I saw you last. I have been anxious to hear how you have been. How can I forget the friendship we shared? You were my best buddy. Do you still remember our crazy arguments about Nietzsche?"

"At the time, you know, I was much infatuated with Nietzsche's shocking idea that God is dead. You were always against my point of view. That was a long time ago, and I am no longer an admirer of Nietzsche. I think he was nothing but a lunatic, speaking in vain. God is not dead. He is still alive and plaguing our fatherland in a manner more deadly than during the time of the Japanese military imperialism. You know, I have become an earnest Communist. I wish the sky and the earth of our fatherland to be painted in a scarlet map. I am confident the day will come sooner rather than later.

"Hey! Hoon! I know you are of wealthy birth. Frankly speaking, I'd like to give you my sincere advice from the bottom of my heart, as your close friend, not as a Communist. You know, the times and tides are changing fast. You have to decide as quickly as possible whether you are going to stay in the north or not. The earlier you make a decision, the better. If you really want to live here in the north, you should fully accept the Communist ideology. If you have no calling to be a true Communist, then forget this place and escape quickly to the south. You go your way, and I will go my way, okay?"

When Young Sup pleaded with his friend, his eyes started getting misty, and he implored his friend, "Hurry up! Hoon! Quickly make a decision, because time is running out."

My father replied, "I really appreciate your friendly advice."

For a moment, Young Sup seemed to have sunk into a pensive reverie. A speechless moment lingered between the two friends. Before long, Young Sup broke the silence. "Hey, Hoon, I must go now. I hope we'll see each other again on the day when our fatherland is reunified. Take care of yourself, so that you should be alive until then, okay?" They sobbed in silence.

My father responded, "Young Sup, please, take care of yourself as well. I'd like to see you again in the near future. "They embraced each other for a moment, and then Young Sup slipped out of his friend's residence quickly and silently, like a bat, into the shadow of darkness.

Young Sup's departure left a great void in my father's heart. He felt the regret of separation mixed with a great loneliness. Even though the two friends had chosen opposite roads, they shared the same thorny destiny under one sky, agonized by their need to pursue different dreams. Young Sup's admonition made Hoon more impatient than ever and more determined to find a way to start his journey south. A thousand emotions swarmed in his mind. What on earth is this Communism about? Is this ideological strife really worth dividing this nation into two pieces and breaking up countless families between the north and the south? Is the 38th parallel a construct of God? No way! That is sheer nonsense! It must be a conspiracy to make a fool of this nation. The abrupt liberation from the Japanese horrors gave birth to another formidable, unwanted malignancy. Ideological and religious insanity began to flood into the country, intoxicating a number of unsophisticated people with an ill-conceived dream and driving innocent masses into a tragic sacrifice, like a herd of cows going to the slaughterhouse. Yoke followed another yoke. He deplored bitterly by himself. All sorts of anxieties connected to gnaw at him. He had a guilty conscience that his elderly parents, who were still living in their hometown of An-Ju City, might be suffering from the radical Communists. Everywhere, life and death seemed to be hanging on the thin thread of fate.

Deepening Regrets

I dwelled deeply about my native place, the formerly peaceful town of An-Ju City, which sits along the Chung-Chun River as it flows strongly with the waters of streams emptying profusely from Myo-Hyang Mountain. As the Siberian Red Wind stormed in, Grandfather was still puzzled over whether he should leave his beloved hometown where his forefathers had lived and been buried.

Early one morning, after he had spent a sleepless night in agony, he rushed to the church, which was situated on a low hill at the entrance to the village. He had served as a senior member of this chapel for a long time. Whenever grandfather was faced with an unmanageable problem, he would run to the church. The chapel had been built with the help of village volunteers immediately after the Korean independence declaration uprising. It was a sanctuary not just for him but for the town, acting as an outpost of a guardian deity, protecting all the villagers. As such, it seemed to command the entrance to the village like a conning tower on a great warship. Grandfather had been born into the family of an obstinate Confucian. However, with the rise of the nationwide independence movement against Japanese control of Korea, my grandfather began to look for solace. After the uprising of March 1, 1919 failed, resulting in the deaths of many innocent victims, he found that solace in a new faith.

He converted to Christianity with no hesitation and devotedly served as a leading member of the church, nurturing his fervent hope that Jesus Christ would deliver this wretched fatherland from the merciless persecution of the Japanese imperialism. Independence, rather than personal salvation, seemed to be the primary goal of his faith. He liked to recite his favorite passage from the Bible:

Blessed are those who hunger and thirst for righteousness, for they will be filled. Blessed are those who are persecuted because of righteousness, for theirs is the kingdom of heaven.
(Matthew 5:6)

The period of thirty-six years under the Japanese military oppression was as hideous and debilitating as though it had lasted a thousand years. In reality, it was like living life as a slave in hell. When the new liberation came, it was greeted as a miracle; people reacted with a frenzied ecstasy bordering on madness. However, the great delight lasted only as long as the foam of a retreating wave. Sinister rumors spread from village to village that the so-called Soviet Liberation Army was advancing in every corner of the northern part of Korea, ravaging cities and villages wherever they went, and hunting for women to rape, regardless of day and night. As the sinister stories spread, there came news of the establishment of a Communist regime, headed by Kim IL Sung, who had strong support from the Soviet forces.

Though Grandfather couldn't comprehend the real meaning

of Communism, he intuitively smelled out an inauspicious atmosphere spreading in his small town. "Another harsh fate is impending," he groaned to himself with a long sigh. During every town emergency, the church bell hanging in the belfry would be rung, resonating through the whole town and reverberating even in the distant sky.

Overcome with an ominous sense of crisis, Grandfather now began to strike the bell fanatically, as if possessed by a spirit, in an effort to call the church members as quickly as possible. "*CLANG! ...CLANG! ...CLANG!*" The bell cried out plaintively as though it were the last voice of many last regrets echoing into the empty heaven. On hearing the toll raising an alarm, the startled villagers responded by flocking hastily into the chapel. A heavy atmosphere reigned as they packed into the church building.

As senior leader of the church, grandfather broke the heavy silence. He spoke cautiously in a subdued voice, "Brothers and sisters, I am really sorry to have alarmed you this morning. But, as you know, our great emancipation from the Japanese invaders seems to have been premature, and it seems that the wheel of fortune has turned against us once more. We gather here this morning to discuss the serious matter of our future path in this era of imminent change. You know that, for more than a quarter of a century together, we have served one God in this peaceful church as brothers and sisters praying with a common heart and a common cause of independence for our fatherland and for our personal salvation. But today, as we now understand, our nation is divided into two, the split being at the 38th parallel, separating us into North and South. The time has clearly come for us to decide, individually, whether to stay in the northern part controlled by the Communist regime, or to go down to the south. I believe that every member of this congregation should choose."

But just as Grandfather was about to continue, one young man in his late thirties sprang up from his seat, screaming in a passion: "Objection! Old comrade! Come down from that pulpit! You are now insulting the great proletarian revolutionary spirit. You are a real sham! Come down! You know, even Jesus was on our side, favoring the proletariat, while He was alive on this earth. The paradise of new sky and new earth will come soon on this northern part of Korea. The bourgeois, such as yourself, should be weeded out. We are all brothers and sisters and have the right to share equal benefits, because we have all suffered too much from the Japanese robbers. Comrade Kim! Get down now! You know, you are a sophisticated deceiver, defiling our whole congregation."

The church was no longer pure and holy. It turned into an arena of ideological combat between brothers. "You are right! You are correct!" was heard throughout the congregation. Screaming and roaring followed in the commotion. The faithful split into two opposing groups. The sons and daughters of God were destined to be part of the bleeding conflict. One group sided with the left wing and the other stood for the right wing. Soon after the violent argument ensued, they cursed one another with hostility. They dragged themselves into the vortex of uncertain historical change, leaving their beloved church as a haunted relic of broken unity, perched on the bleak hill of their village. As they walked away, the distant sound of the church bell, carried on the wind, was heard like an echo of a passing dream. As time passed by, my grandfather's tenant farmers vanished one by one, without giving notice.

One evening, an unexpected visitor knocked on grandfather's

door. "Master! Master!" It was the familiar voice of a domestic servant who had worked for grandfather for many years. Instead of his usual garb, the man wore a black Lenin suit, though he showed the same politeness as in the past. He calmly paid his respects to his former master, yet grandfather sensed things were different. His speech was delivered in a cold voice tinted with an unmistakable touch of arrogance. "Master! As you know, the present political situation is very serious. It might be dangerous for you to stay. I think you should leave this town before dawn. This is the last time I will be able to give you advice, and I do it now only in consideration of your having cared for my family, in the past, as if we had been your own." Later, this former servant became a Communist to the core, rising to a senior position in the local Communist party. "Remember! Master! Time is of the essence. If you hesitate in your decision, you might be tried in a people's court. Please, hurry up, Master!" Grandfather was puzzled, but nodded his head anyway. After that, his former servant never showed his face again.

Grandfather, in his advanced age, was suddenly reduced to a homeless wanderer. Not only had he lost all that he had accumulated in his lifetime, but his family had been separated as well. The cataclysmic Red Storm ruined his life, taking his wishes and hopes away in a puff of smoke. He recalled the story of Job from the Old Testament, and the unbearable hardships that Job faced in the test for his faithfulness. Grandfather began to wonder whether he should cling to his faith in the face of God's capricious ways. Tears welled up in his withered eyes. He set out toward the south, searching for an uncertain refuge.

As time passed, his regrets deepened with each passing day and night. At last, in the late fall of 1948, he barely succeeded in crossing the 38th parallel and reaching the southern soil. A cloud of red dragonflies was soaring up into the evening sky. In contrast with the dismal atmosphere of the northern part of Korea, which was twisting in a political hurricane, the atmosphere of the south seemed brisk and free. Some natives of the southern part called refugees from the north, *Sam-Pal Taragy* meaning, "homeless beggars who crossed the 38th parallel from the north."

The first refuge where our family settled was a cozy and antiquated town called Tapgol-Seung-Bang, which means, "monks' chamber where the stone pagoda was erected." It was situated in the outskirts of the capital city of Seoul. Inhabitants of the town were born with a conservative inclination, and most of them were sympathetic with the new migrants from the north. *"Piyang-Gip! Piyang-Gip!"* The villagers used to call us a nickname that sounds similar to the pronunciation of Pyeung-Yang, the capital city of North Korea. My eldest uncle's family joined with our family. The two families lived in the same house with two small rooms that had barely enough space for all our bodies. Youngsters wiggled about in a swarm, as children do in orphanages. Though the circumstances of the refugee life were hard and scanty, the kids looked happy, hustling about without a hint of woe clouding their faces.

The tragedy of upheaval originally fell most heavily on the adults. However, the oldest sons of the two families were instantly drafted into labor. My cousin Chang, who was six years older than me, and I began taking odd jobs in order for our families to survive. My cousin Chang carried around his neck an open wooden box packed with white sticks of taffy. I followed at my cousin's heel, as a loyal subordinate, calling: "*Yeut sacio! Yeut sacio!*" meaning, "please buy taffy."

As we were strolling about the Chung-Ryangni railroad station square in the late fall of 1948, we found a number of soldiers standing in queues, waiting for the special military train headed for the front line at the 38th parallel. We approached them quietly, breaking through their long lines. "Uncle!" (which refers to a man of one's parents' age), "*Yeut sacio!*" We began to yell out, hoping to receive a tiny profit, but our expectations were utterly shattered on the spot. A stout soldier among them had sprung up abruptly from the row and kicked the small, dingy box which was clinging to my cousin's slender neck. He then began to mercilessly trample the taffy sticks that were tumbling all about on the dusty ground. He cursed at us, "Get lost! Rats! *Bal-Geng-Ei-Seki!*" (meaning, "son of the Communist"). His words were shooting out of his mouth like bullets spitting out of a machine gun. We ran away and hid and waited until the soldiers left the railroad station. "Damn it! I lost everything," Chang grumbled, feeling anger and humiliation. "Bad luck, isn't it?" His face became red and heated from his shame and wrath, but as we were walking home, the cool autumn wind gently blew on his face, soothing his rage and calming his emotions. Evidently, our business venture was not much help to the family anyway, and immediately after that incident, the family gave up the struggling taffy business.

As time passed, the town of Tapgol-Seung-Bang bewitched me, intoxicating me with a mysterious scent constantly wafting through the village. Nestled in the bosom of a relatively low mountain, which formed a backdrop to the south, was an antiquated Buddhist temple called Bomunsa. From a fountainhead in the mountain, a crystal stream trickled down all year long, never drying up. The temple would lead me into an ethereal world where a mystical aroma assailed my nostrils, enveloping my soul in a somewhat somber mood. The believers were praying with their hands pressed together, and they were burning incense in front of the Buddha images. This was so that their beloved flesh and blood would ascend to the heavens above. There were also nuns, who were beating wood blocks in a monotonous tune. The rosy complexions of the nuns and the sad looks of the believers captivated me. The temple became not only my sole playful diversion but also my first spiritual sanctuary.

In addition, on a special occasion such as the day of the Buddha's coming, the whole village rolled in a festival atmosphere with countless shaded lamps illuminating every corner of the temple buildings, and the humming sound of nuns chanting Sutra text. The nuns performed a Buddhist dance, with muffled steps, to the sound of the gong. The scene would cause me to choke up, as it exerted an unexplainable influence over me. Indeed, the whole village seethed until dusk in an agitated, yet festive mood on the Buddha's birthday. As a last sequence of the festival, all the monks of the temple would appear in special robes and make the rounds of the village in long queues, chanting the Sutra in concert with a performance on Buddhist musical instruments. The ringing of the gong and the song from the flute were a supplication for the village's peace. Then, the festival would reach its climax. A bunch of excited kids were apt to wander about, tagging at priests' heels in a clamor. I mingled with them until night closed upon the scene.

"*Ting-Ting-Ting-a-Ling!!*" Early every morning the subdued sound of the Buddhist temple's bell would awaken the town from its dreams. The holy Buddha played an important role in the lives of many of the villagers. Some of the villagers were beset by sufferings from intolerable adversities; in particular, those who had lost their blood due to diseases would sometimes hire a shaman, called a Mudanq. These villagers would turn to this traditional Korean folk-faith, hoping to either heal their illnesses or comfort the spirits of the deceased. "*Gong... Gong...Go...n...g...*"

Amid the uproarious sounds of the gong, the sorceress would perform a hair-raising rite: dancing, raving, and muttering to herself something incomprehensible, as though possessed by spirits and beset by hallucinations. "Out! Out! Ghost out!" she shouted spasmodically at random in order to push out the evil spirits from the sick. She also called the name of the dead, in order to invoke the soul of the deceased. At the height of this frenzied exorcism, the shaman would hit the gong more madly than ever. The witch would bring her voice to a high shrieking pitch. In the end, the spirit of the dead would possess the body of the shaman, and she would start to whimper uncontrollably, reeling off the regrets of the dead person. Then the survivors would burst into a bitter wail as though they had been face-to-face with the departed, beloved one.

As the bizarre ritual was winding down, the person who had employed the conjurer would begin to hand out rice cakes. They were piled on a low wooden table that had been set in the middle of the ritual site, in anticipation of feeding the spectators who crowded into the house. That intense ritual with the shaman would replay in my dreams, sending a chill down my spine.

The exorcising held me spellbound. In the town of Tapgol-Seung-Bang, both the Buddha and the shaman coexisted in harmony. In addition to the shaman's arena and the Buddha's holy precincts, I enjoyed loitering around the open market close to the village, in search of free food. There was this old man with an old, conventional popping machine that was stuffed with dried corn grains which, when heated and churned, would eventually turn into white, puffy popcorn, which then spewed into a deep, long, iron net basket. Once in a while, a popped corn would escape through one of the holes. Like a cat focusing its eyes on a rat's hole, I concentrated my entire attention on catching the very moment when some of the popcorn would burst out of the holes and, after making a short flight in the open air, fall down on the dusty ground. I would then pick up the popcorn, dust it off, and pop it into my mouth. This would put me in a state of sweet ecstasy.

One day, while tagging along after mother, I had a chance to attend a Sunday Bible school. The church did a great thing for the children by providing them with soft rice cakes and sweet cookies. Shortly after this first encounter with Sunday school, I began to feel that this place was a precinct of grace that was saving me from hunger. I then began to look forward to every Sunday morning. Shortly thereafter, it dawned on me that I had to share this special blessing with the other children in my town who were in need. I made up my mind to become a special evangelist for the truth of rice cakes. "Hey! You!" I would yell. "Why don't you come with me? The church gives sweet rice cakes free of charge. " My tempting offer to other children my age raised their spirits high. "Really? Free? You sure?" My young friends reacted right away, swallowing their excitement. My offer was a hit and many were allured by the charity. With such a small bit of bait, the young, innocent kids were easily caught, one by one. My first missionary work was a great success.

However, my holy ministry was suddenly cut short by a skin infection. There was a rash all over my body and, as time went by, the itching grew worse. Nothing seemed to work on relieving the skin rash. As a last resort, an unidentified, stinky ointment was plastered thickly over my entire body. I was then wrapped in old newspapers, which only added another element of aggravation to my pain. Every night, my body and soul writhed in a hellish pit of despair. The more I scratched on the rashes, the more scabs developed on my body. Repeated scratching caused the scabs to peel off and bleed. Ironically, the bleeding relieved me momentarily from the unbearable itch. I felt this rash to be a curse, karma for some unknown sin I had done in my former life. This skin infection lasted for almost a year. Then, I began my first year in elementary school.

In March of 1950, I started at Dong-Shin elementary school. It took about half an hour by foot to get to the school from our town of Tapgol-Seung-Bang. On both sidewalks leading to the school, at regular intervals, were verdant poplar trees oozing spring sap. As I would walk along the lanes under the canopy of trees, the rays of the morning sun would filter through their delicate foliage, providing a tinge of light. The refreshing spring smell charmed me with a buoyant feeling. These were splendid, carefree days in my life.

However, this feeling did not last long. An ominous dark cloud seemed to be looming over the Korean peninsula. Radio reports blasted alarming news that the military conflict on the 38th parallel continued to escalate throughout the region and spilled over into southern Korea. The bloody clashes between the left and right wings became more and more frequent. The bright springtime was turning into a somber season of apprehension.

One day, my youngest uncle, who was a medical student at a university in a local city, appeared in the town of Tapgol-

Seung-Bang, where his parents resided. His left cheek was deeply cut and his right hand bandaged. It was clear that something serious must have happened to him. His father pressed him for an explanation.

"One afternoon," my uncle said, "all of the students gathered in a large university auditorium to discuss important issues regarding student activities. Soon after the general assembly commenced, the students split into two parts: the right wing, and the left wing, yelling and jeering at each other. At times, their clash developed into a blood-shedding fight. In the middle of the chaos, a sharp knife from a left-wing student hit my left cheek. I feel lucky to be alive." Newspapers reported that, on the military demarcation line, skirmishes were taking place more frequently than ever.

The last days of May 1950 came and went, and the fragrance of the acacia flowers became overwhelming. Cicadas hidden between the branches of the acacia trees were crying in a shrill chirrup. Toward the end of June 1950, my uncle showed up again with his face tanned, wearing an army uniform that had badges of second lieutenant on both shoulders.

"Father!" he exclaimed. "I have volunteered for service. I just dropped by to say farewell to you before going to the front line. You know, the Yang Yang district, close to the 38th parallel" He stammered and his head drooped a little. His father became numb while his mother broke out in muted sobs. "Father! Mother! Don't worry about me, I will be back soon. I think sooner or later, the unification will happen. Then, we can go back to our hometown. Please take care of your health until I come back again to see you, ok?" Before he left, uncle turned around and said to me, "Hey nephew! When I come home, I am going to buy lots of cake for you, okay?" He left his beloved parents, never to return again. Seeing my teary-eyed uncle leaving for the last time is one of the saddest memories that I carry with me to this day.

The War

"*Clang...Clang...Clang.*" It was a crystal-clear Sunday morning on June 25th, 1950. The church bell was tolling sonorously with a deep, rich sound. As on every Sunday, I followed my mother on her way to church. This particular morning, for no apparent reason, I happened to join the service for adults instead of attending the Sunday school for children. The rays of the morning sun, filtering through the windowpanes of the church, dazzled me. Before the sermon was delivered, two violinists were performing along with a pianist, playing a sentimental tune. They played a hymn titled, "Nearer, My God, to Thee."

Nearer, my God, to thee, nearer to thee!
E 'en though it be a cross that raiseth me,
Still all my song shall be, Nearer, my God, to thee,
Nearer, my God, to thee, nearer to thee, Amen.

The psalm created a sense of sadness, providing an ominous presentiment that something grave was impending in days to come.

On that Sunday afternoon, villagers of Tapgol-Seung-Bang were making an unusual stir of activity. Talk about war was whispered from one anxious villager to the next. One villager, who had a ghostly look of fear on his face, was heard saying that early that morning, the North Communist Army had pushed through the 38th parallel. They were already coming closer to us. Young men in green uniforms could be seen running about. "All soldiers! Return to your respective units immediately!" the military police yelled through their bullhorns from their jeeps, as people ran screaming through the streets. At short intervals, the siren blew in the air of the capital city, Seoul, heralding national emergency. Then, a couple of silvery airplanes appeared in the sky, as if providing an airshow. Whenever these flying metallic objects emerged from the clouds, the people in the streets scattered in a wink, scurrying to find shelter. The government sought to reassure Seoulites through continual radio broadcasts:

"Our National Defense Army is fighting bravely against the Communist invader. Please stay calm." However, Russian Yak fighter planes connected to make frequent appearances, popping in and out over Seoul. Concurrently, amidst the uproar of the suspicious air objects, the siren howled and started echoing throughout the city. Enveloped in horror, villagers began to evacuate in haste. Our family was kept awake, listening to a weird rumble from afar. Father inexplicably disappeared.

As my family joined the southbound evacuees the following morning, an ashy cloud was hanging oppressively over the village. Our oxcart, loaded with the family's belongings, clattered along the dusty road. My youngest brother dangled from the top of the bundle. He squealed with evident satisfaction as the rest of our flock trudged along in the shadow of the cart. The old ox was panting as if beyond its ability.

As night descended, our southward migration was suddenly blocked. The bridge that we needed to cross had been destroyed. The National Defense forces had blasted the bridge just after the President of the Republic of South Korea, Syngman Rhee, fled the capital city, leaving most of the Seoulites under the rule of the Communist occupation forces. You could hear some curse the President, "God damn! Just like Judas, who betrayed his master, *he* betrays his own people." A rumor spread that many people had been crossing the bridge when the National Defense forces used their powerful explosions to blow it up. Thousands of would-be evacuees were buried in the Han River.

While we lingered around the destroyed Han bridge, morning dawned upon us. "Let's go back to Tapgol-Seung-Bang. There is no way to escape and no choice but to return to the village," mother said with a resigned weariness. As we retreated through the downtown streets of a newly-occupied Seoul City, red flags fluttered on every corner. Heavy Russian tanks, decorated in red flags, rolled aggressively over the main streets, while army trucks kicked up clouds of dust on the side streets. Having captured the city, the Communist army was carrying out a pacification activity by distributing sweet cookies to children and passersby. "Hey! Kid! Take these cookies!" a young Communist soldier said to me as he handed over a couple of pieces. Deeply impressed with this unexpected gift from the Communist Santa Claus, I tasted the crispy sweets, biting off the corners of the cookies bit by bit, savoring my treasure. A somber, Communist military song was being heard throughout the city:

Marks of blood on every range of the Jangbeck Mountain
Marks of blood on every stream of Amnok River

Still blooming over the liberal Korea
These holy marks shed bright rays
Oh dear is the name, our beloved general
Oh glorious is the name, General Kim IL Sung!

As we reached the town of Tapgol-Seung-Bang, it was obvious that the village had already been dyed "Red." A large banner strewn across the top of the police box, which stood as a sentry at the mouth of the town, greeted us with a high-handed wave. An army of small flags waved from the gate of every house. The sight of all the red flags made the hair on the back of my neck stand on end. Before the war broke out, a little girl named Sora had lived next door to us. Her mother would often drop by our residence to have a chat with my mother. Though my mother knew nothing of the background of Sora's mother, the woman and my mother became very close. Sora's mother never mentioned anything about her husband, and nobody in the village knew her true colors. A vague rumor circulated throughout the village that her husband was a Communist and had been shot to death by the police. However, by her appearance, she was always bright with no shadow on her face.

Upon our return to the village, after our failure in crossing the Han River, Sora's mother came scurrying to our door. Her face was bright, as usual, but her tone was somewhat contemptuous. "Where have you been?" she asked. Mother stammered unintelligibly, with a baffled look. "Ah, don't worry, that's okay, I'm just asking!" She did not seem disturbed by mother's feeble answer. On the contrary, she seemed pleased, as though it confirmed her suspicions that we were born to the bourgeoisie and had fled North Korea. On the other hand, my mother had no interest in revealing her political identity at all, because she considered Sora's mother a warm-hearted neighbor. Every time she would stop by for a chat, her daughter, Sora, would take after her mother. Sora was a shy girl who would play by herself, hanging about the shady corner of our house. On the occasions that she accidentally came face-to-face with me, she would quickly drop her head in order to avoid my eyes.

Sora had a clean, round face and large, black eyes. She looked like a tiny wildflower that somehow had grown without being contaminated by the dirt of the world. Even though I attempted to catch a chance to address her, she kept away from my gaze, in her shyness. *Sora.* What a beautiful name, what sparkling eyes! It dawned upon me that she had a legendary name that meant: *"dreaming in the profound sea forever."* After the war broke out, I never saw Sora again.

Shortly after the Communist army had taken over the village, Sora's mother began to reveal her true colors. She quickly became the head of the local women's committee. There was no doubt that she must have been a secret Communist agent who had been implanted in the south before the outbreak of the war. One night, Sora's mother made an abrupt visit to our house. Her unexpected arrival stunned my mother for a moment. It was almost as if a messenger from another world had popped in, and, while they talked, it seemed that the whole town was enveloped in a deathlike silence. "I may not come back to see you again," Sora's mother said. "As you know, I am now busy with my new mission for the revolutionary activity. Don't worry; I am still your friend. I would like to help you, friend, but I must go now. Take care of yourself. So long." Sora's mother whispered in a gentle voice. After their talk, she vanished.

Despite the warm solace, mother was seized with the fear

that Sora's mother might bring charges against our family. The times and tides seemed fickle. It felt as if the fate of our family might be suspended on the tip of her finger. During the wartime, God seemed to be powerless; Communists replaced the Almighty and became the absolute power. The reverberating sounds from the temple, the shaman's lunatic utterances, the resounding chimes of the church, and the boisterous voices of small children, were no longer heard. The Buddha, shaman, and even Christ, were all gone from the sphere of the town of Tapgol-Seung-Bang. The Communist God became the sole deity. General Kim IL Sung was worshipped fanatically as their living God. The villagers holed up in their houses with extreme caution, for fear that something inauspicious might happen to them. I, too, spent many sleepless nights listening to the sound of cannons booming from afar. The sound was like the rumble of an approaching storm.

By day, the village was relatively quiet. However, as night fell, the town began to buzz and a dismal atmosphere descended. There was a feeling that a tragic human drama was likely to unfold. Sora's mother was no longer seen in public. We trembled in terror that our family might be one of the first targets, since we had fled from the north. Mother was in constant fear that a strange man might show up at our doorstep. With the approach of midnight, their tracking of the so-called reactionary elements would reach a peak. Then, the sound of wailing would reach my ears. Through the wispy holes of the worn-out wooden fence of my house, I would catch a glimpse of people being led away with their hands tied behind their backs. As they trudged along the narrow alley in single file, they whimpered bitterly. Night after night, the Red agents kept on searching for their prey. The families of police officers and National Defense Army members were categorized as the worst type of reactionaries. Our peaceful town had been turned into an inferno. The pitiful villagers were left to be engulfed in an inescapable labyrinth of despair. The compassion of Buddha and the omnipotence of God seemed to fade. The occupation forces and the village people played cruel games of hide and seek with each other. The comforting Buddhist fragrance that had once wafted over the whole village had been replaced by a dense smell of blood.

As feared, late one evening, two men dressed in the Communist garb broke into our house. "Any men in this house?" they asked, as they searched every nook and cranny. One of the two men glared at my mother, pressing her for an answer.

"Nobody but women and children," my mother responded in a voice choked with fear.

"Where is your husband now?" they demanded.

"I don't know where he is," my mother moaned.

This first visit was not their last. In addition to these periodic raids, the adults of the village were sometimes called to the police box at the town's entrance. These nocturnal meetings were meant to indoctrinate the Communist ideology into the innocent villager's minds. The speeches were usually lengthy and tedious. "We are now fighting the glorious national liberation war. You know, our great People's Army will accomplish our task shortly. *Man-Se!* Long live General Kim IL Sung! *Man-Se!*" People had to mimic these actions by clapping their hands and singing war songs like possessed idiots. The nightly hunt for quarry was relentless. The desperate wail of the victims was a constant source of distress.

"We are in danger of being dragged away in the purge. Why is this awful thing happening to us?" Mother flared up, "This is worse than the Japanese occupation. Everybody is going mad."

Red Dragonflies

It was a hot and humid evening when somebody pounded on the front gate. The entire family jumped in fear. "Who are you?" asked mother in a shaky voice.

"Open the gate! I am a messenger from your relative. Let me come in first, and then I will explain." The man barged in as though he were afraid he was being followed. "Please move quickly! I have to slip out of here undetected with your two children, before dawn."

My grandmother quickly cooked some emergency food for my cousin, Chang, and myself. She baked soybeans with a dash of salt in a large black kettle. The aroma from the cooking filled the house.

"Get up! Get up!" mother said, while shaking me from a sound sleep.

"What's the matter? Let me sleep!" I growled.

Grandmother tied a plump pouch of roasted beans onto my waist, and a pouch also onto Chang's waist. Just before daybreak, under the cover of darkness, the messenger, accompanied by two young children, snuck out of the village like stealthy night mice. I followed close behind the messenger. The darkness drew me to its breast and I felt snug and secure in the obscurity of the night. As we fled the town of Tapgol¬Seung-Bang, the sky was dawning. The shadow of men wriggling on the bare street, and the Red Communist flags flapping in the morning fog, tickled my visual senses.

We three fugitives proceeded to an unknown place. "Where are we going now?" I moaned. The messenger ignored my complaining. The road to nowhere felt endless. The scorching sun seemed to be cremating everything in its path. The blisters on my feet made me hobble.

"Let's have a break here," our guide bluntly uttered. I flopped down in dog-tiredness under the shade of a large, solitary Zelkova tree, on a low hill a few paces from the main road. I stretched my legs on the dusty ground. When I pulled off my shoes, a foul-smelling steam arose, cooling off my feet. I took a fistful of baked soybeans out of the small bag that clung to my waist. I chewed the roasted beans until I had mashed them into a paste, and let the processed food slowly seep down my throat. A swarm of ants that had been working around the root of the Zelkova tree attacked my stinking feet. They marched up and down my pale shin, tickling my skin. I let them enjoy their wayward toying with my smelly feet. The road leading north looked deserted. At times, army trucks loaded with the Red People's soldiers would come and go, raising clouds of yellow dust in their wake.

While we took a short rest, two strangers heading north invaded part of our shade. A man dressed in Communist attire took a deep puff from his cigarette. The other man had a rope firmly tied around him. He looked up at the empty sky with his pale face. There was no dialogue between the man who held the rope and the man who was tied by it. I was curious to know what their story was about. They refused to even make eye contact with any of us. Just as I was about to pass out from exhaustion, the messenger's thin voice fell on my ears. "Let's go, kids, get up!" He gently urged me to go, patting me on my back.

"BOOooom...BOOoooom!" The distant thunder of guns reminded me of the sad reality in a surreal world. The faces of my father and youngest uncle momentarily flickered through my mind; "Are they alive or dead? Where are they now?" Drifting into a somber mood, I pondered their fate.

"Hurry up kids! We have a destination to reach before dark."

Limping along with my cousin, I complained, "Why on earth are we on this dubious journey?" I murmured in vain.

Upon reaching the foot of the So-Yo Mountain, the evening sun painted the sky crimson as if it were glowing with its last gasp of passion. As we arrived at the entrance of a small village, we noticed groups of straw-thatched houses. A boy in his early teens came out to greet us. "My name is Hyeung Jin. Come with me, your old uncle is waiting for you," the boy said, brightly. Having fulfilled his responsibility, the messenger left. Sporadic gunshots were heard at irregular intervals. The boy walked a few paces ahead of us. We walked along a meandering mountain trail that was heavily lined with chestnut trees. The canopy of trees held a teeming throng of Communist soldiers seeking to camouflage themselves from air attacks.

One of the soldiers spoke to me in a coaxing way, "Hey kid! Where are you going?"

"We are just going over there, sir," I mumbled vaguely while pointing aimlessly.

"This is a tiger's nest, not a place to be seeking shelter," my cousin muttered. As we progressed up the mountain, we could see less and less, until we saw nothing and could only listen to the chorus of nameless, chirping insects, as well as the occasional howling of wild creatures. I pushed through the dense wooded area as quickly as I could in order to keep up with the boy who was leading us. I was terrified of being left behind. It was a horrible night of climbing. As we rose to the crest of the mountain, a small hermit's retreat came into sight. It was tucked into a recess of the mountain in absolute solitude. The forlorn cottage that had once housed a succession of anchorites became the terminal station for two young pilgrims seeking solace from the war.

Under the cover of night, my eldest uncle would suddenly appear out of nowhere. He would then disappear just as quickly, like a phantom of the night. He said that he concealed himself in a deep cavern, changing his hiding place from time to time. As the days dragged on, the emergency food of parched beans that my grandmother had provided me was depleted. The first pangs of hunger began to gnaw at my gut. Out of fear of starvation, my cousin, Chang, proposed an idea. "I think each of us should be responsible for finding his own food, okay?" he said.

I began to wander about in the heart of the mountain like a feral animal, searching for anything edible. Once, when I was busily picking wild mountain berries, I ran away at the sight of a large, black snake, slithering in the bush. After that incident, I had recurring nightmares about this huge, black serpent that would chase me, until I woke up in horror. This nightmare haunted me for a very long time.

My search for food led me in many directions. I followed a creek that wound its way down from the top of the mountain, unrolling at a wide, flat field. In one corner of that plain was a small bean plot. I would make my way to the bean patch by crawling and creeping along as though I were practicing military guerrilla tactics. When I would infiltrate deep into the bean field, I would lie flat on my back in a narrow space of ditch that ran between the ridges that had been planted with beans. Thus buried among the dense bean plants, I could lie at ease and chew the tender raw beans, much as a cow would, without the fear of being detected. Lying among the beans, I would look up at the white clouds sailing peacefully across the blue sky, and a sense of euphoria would build up in me. I felt released from all the ambiguous fears that the world had to offer, even if only for a short time. I wished that the felicitous moment could last for eternity. However, every time I glutted myself with the wild beans, I would, without fail, suffer from diarrhea, bringing me back to harsh reality. After those bouts of discomfort, I would lay my worn-out body among the beans and conjure up the days when I used to enjoy savory rice cakes at Sunday school.

Once, after throwing myself down on the earth and shivering in half-sleeplessness, a successive cracking of guns reverberated in my ears. I lay as still as a corpse, and a swallowtail flew above me, gently flapping its colorful wings, frolicking to and fro. An army of unidentified insects began to assault my entire body. I was indifferent to their wild raid and let them gnaw at my worn-out flesh. Survival seemed to be doubtful. If I were not alive, the pain might not exist in this world or the next. It occurred to me that a piece of bread could have priority over everything. I was dying to eat a bowl of hot steamed rice. At this point I was convinced that food was not only life, but also truth. I reflected that it would be nice if God should place more importance on the present than on an optimistic future.

To become a survivor in the vortex of wartime, I had to prowl the mountain like a stray wolf. I had to become part of the natural landscape. Instinct took over. I ceased to contemplate the dignity of man. I chose to become a savior for myself, because in extreme starvation, neither ideology, nor God, offers any redemption. As time passed by, I accepted the laws of survival of the fittest. I became a mole, digging out potatoes hidden under the ground, or a squirrel, cracking acorns to get the nut within. All the creatures of the mountain became my partners for survival.

As September approached, the sound of gunfire grew more frequent. Fighter planes emerged in formation at short intervals above the So-Yo Mountain. Occasionally, fighter bombers would swoop down the valley to ferret out the People's soldiers, as a hawk would hunt for mice in the same fields. The ear-splitting boom of the jets seemed to mimic the screech of that majestic bird. Making things even more ominous were the Communist soldiers who had swarmed under the chestnut trees, now incinerated where they fell. There was a sensation in the air that something was likely to happen soon. As September 1950 drew to a close, the trees changed into their autumn outfits. The tinted leaves brought a flicker of color that was ignited by the mountain wind. At the summit of Mount So-Yo, the only indications of human habitation were the shadows of two wild boys who had adapted themselves to the mountain and their old uncle's irregular appearances.

One afternoon I happened upon a stranger who popped up at my retreat without any warning. "Have you been visited by any adults?" he questioned me, scrutinizing the cottage. I was afraid the stranger might smell the presence of my uncle.

"No, sir, I have not seen anybody."

As it turned out, my fear was unfounded. During my three-month exile in So-Yo Mountain, I became acquainted with many of the natives who lived there. All the creatures of the mountain were my companions. When the mountain magpie, with its shiny, blue feathers, flew into my lonesome hut, my heart would beat quickly and I was sure it was a good omen. But when a treacherous mountain raven would caw from the top of my grass roof, a feeling of uneasiness would overcome me. Amongst all of the creatures that called upon my mountaintop hermitage, the red dragonflies were my special friends. I was especially happy to see them at sunset, when all of creation was bathed in the evening glow. The red dragonflies would often use the twig fences surrounding my hermitage as a resting stop on their flight into the western sky. Some would also land on the thatched roof, but the majority of these winged creatures would touch down on the tips of the loose bush clover. That was when my playfulness would come into action.

I would approach with caution, seeking an opportunity to grab the quivering tail of the dragonfly between my thumb and index finger. As I drew closer, the creature would continue to roll its tiny head, with its blurred eyes, from side to side, keeping me in its sight. Its body would tremble spontaneously with the movement of its glassy wings, and the supple tail would curl up and down, as if it were a supersonic feeler. Most often the dragonfly would take off before I was able to grab the little beast. When I was lucky enough to succeed in holding onto the tiny tail, the dragonfly would struggle to free itself from my fingers by vibrating its transparent wings and convulsing its whole body. Then I would tie a tiny thread of long straw onto the space of the body between the wings and the tail. Then I would let it fly into the air. I would watch the red dragonfly, tied with a long straw cord, soar up into heaven until it looked like a speck of dust.

In spite of my ceaseless molestation, the red dragonflies continued to fly into my retreat and visit me in the evening glow. It seemed to me that they also liked to play a game of hide and seek with great affinity. When the red dragonflies ascended to the heavens as angels of peace, I would become one of them, rising up into the distant sky. The dragonflies became my great friends, swarming about my isolation in the twilight of my childhood.

One day, as I toiled, hunting for food, occasionally seeing my uncle, and playing with red dragonflies, a squadron of bombers began making successive appearances. These became more and more frequent. When I heard the wild roar of those planes, I ran to the crest of the mountain where I would have a view of the bombing of distant downtown Uijonbu-City. Lying face down on the stony ground at the crown of the mountain, I enjoyed a panoramic view of the bombers' air show. At the very moment the fighter planes were above me, they started their perpendicular dive toward their downtown targets. Shortly after their vertical dive, the blasting sounds of the bombs could be heard. The bombings produced black clouds, and after all the bombings had taken place, the planes ascended into the air in a fork formation. The thrilling aerial pageant was re-enacted many times each day. The rude metal birds, without fail, would come over my sanctuary while I played with the peacemakers, the red dragonflies. The thundering noise of the fighter bombers created a contrast with the serene gestures of the red dragonflies. Through all this mayhem, autumn continued to ripen, painting the leaves with gold and red strokes.

Ebb and Flow

Early one evening, toward the close of September 1950, I happened to call on my grandmother, who had been staying in a grass-roofed village close by the road. As darkness set in on the small village, a band of Communist soldiers, who were showing signs of fatigue, swept into the rural community. After being in the village for a short time, one of the soldiers asked my grandmother to cook their dinner for them. He produced some raw rice from their military bags for her to cook. "Grandmother! Sooner or later we will all be dead, so tonight's supper may be our last meal. Please, cook this rice for us. You look like my mother..." They begged in a polite manner, as if they were imploring sons.

"Don't worry, kids, I will cook for you. I have a son your age." They sat in a circle around my grandmother's small room and ate quickly.

"Thank you, grandmother. Please live until our fatherland will be reunified." One of the soldiers, not yet in his twenties, had tears rolling down his face. They left in reluctance as if they departed from their own mothers.

Early the next morning, after the Communist soldiers

had departed for a destiny unknown, I stumbled upon an extraordinary scene. A company of a different group of Communist soldiers were lining up in rows of four at the branch of a muddy main road that forked to the north and to the south. The commander yelled and the soldiers followed, quickly retiring down the northern fork of the road. The roaring of heavy artillery could be heard moving closer and closer. It seemed that something strange was in the air. As dawn turned into day, I noticed that many people were descending from the mountains. These people had taken refuge, like bats, in the caves of So-Yo Mountain for almost three months. They now had the confidence to show their faces in the light of day. *"Man-se! Man-se!"* ("Live ten thousand years!") Their shouts of relief echoed in the shadows of Mount So-Yo. My eldest uncle also appeared in broad daylight. His haggard face was full of thick hair, as if he had turned into a beast. The new tide was flowing in like a cataclysmic change. "Look at the giant soldiers! Those big noses!" people clamored in surprise. I thought that the big soldiers with white faces must have come from another planet. US Army jeeps were carrying captured Communist officers as prisoners in the backseats, rolling down the dusty road.

"US forces have taken back Seoul City!" my uncle cried in high spirits. "Let's go back to Tapgol-Seung-Bang. We will be safe there."

The road to Seoul City was bustling with throngs of refugees. We were like a caravan of gypsies sharing the same uncertain destiny as we made the long procession toward Seoul. As we migrated southward, we came upon an unmarked street corner where a number of US soldiers were resting. Some sat on their military bags, while some were lying on the bare ground.

"American soldiers!" somebody among the crowd shouted at them. "Hey! Kid!" a young American soldier with pink cheeks turned to look at me. As I turned to look at him, he threw a shower of presents at me which included chewing gum and various other kinds of treats. Luckily, I was able to catch a thin chocolate bar and a piece of spearmint gum. The taste of the sweet chocolate left a strong impression on me.

While walking along the road leading to the capital city of Seoul, I was stunned from time to time by the horrible sight of several dead American soldiers. The image of one young American GI particularly shocked me. He was in his late teens, lying dead in a ditch along the street. Insects were assaulting his body. A cloud of black flies licked at his rotting face while a colony of ants climbed onto his corpse. The terrible image of this dead soldier is forever burned into the recesses of my memory. Why should this young man die? This was my first understanding of true tragedy. Refugees sluggishly moved southward. The UN military police and Republic of Korea (ROK) MP often stopped the shabby-looking refugees and rummaged through whatever bundles they had in their possession. Their IDs were also meticulously looked over, all in an effort to find anything that might link these souls to the Communists.

It was late afternoon when we returned to the village of Tapgol-Seung-Bang. The red flags and Communist soldiers who had occupied the village were nowhere to be seen. They had been replaced by fresh flags of South Korea, and one could hear the sounds of young children clamoring in the streets. I quickly joined the other children. The town seemed to be brisk again. The ringing of the church bells could also be heard again. The villagers did their best to continue leading their lives as if nothing had happened. However, every part of the village held traces of the ravages of war. Many horrible rumors were running rampant throughout the town. One was that an old man, who had lived next door to us before the war, had been shot to death on the spot for stealing a sack of rice from a Communist Army's warehouse. As the Communist Army withdrew from the town, many people had been thrown alive into the deep public well, while others had been kidnapped to the north. I was most curious to know what had happened to my little girlfriend, Sora. It was said that Sora's mother had gone with her daughter, concurrently with the retreat of the Communist Army from the town. I was never able to find out exactly what had happened to Sora. The little angel must have become a victim of the ideological war between the north and the south. Was she alive or dead? I missed Sora then, and to this day her dear memory is intermingled with a heartbreaking sorrow.

It was a crisp afternoon in late autumn of 1950. The children of the village were playing soccer in an open space. A poor-looking man with deep-set eyes came close to me, calling my name. He was my father, who had been gone since the day the war broke out. We stared at each other, speechless. In fact, his return struck the whole family dumb. We had presumed that he was dead, and yet he came walking back into our lives! "Where have you been?" my mother asked. "How did you survive?"

Father began to describe his ordeal: "It was awful. The morning war broke out, I received an urgent message from my old army academy. I was immediately ordered into battle. I had no time to think, let alone catch my breath. My unit was very poorly armed and the north Communists were equipped with heavy Russian tanks. It was as if an egg were fighting a rock. We were hopelessly out-armed. I saw many young soldiers falling down, screaming; some were blown apart and their blood smeared across the ground. I was so scared, I couldn't collect my thoughts. It was a hellish war game. Many soldiers died unnecessarily. In the frenzy of the fight I lost track of time and space. I miraculously found myself sent back to the rear. I was discharged due to a wound I received from battle."

In the meantime, there was no news from my youngest uncle. He had been sent to the front, close to the 38th parallel, about a month before the war broke out. His parents waited anxiously for his return. It was rumored that his military unit had been totally wiped out on the day when the Communist Army had launched an overall attack against the south, crossing the 38th military demarcation. There were no survivors and no trace of any of the division members. Their bodies must have melted down into the earth or vanished into the ether. There were no bodies, and no graves. Though the capital city, Seoul, was repatriated, the stink of war hung to it. Silvery B-29 bombers would turn up in the skies of Seoul. When the planes appeared, I would bury myself under a thick quilt, or dig a hole in an empty space under the floorboards. The war between the north and south seemed to flow back and forth across the 38th parallel.

A Mass Evacuation

As the new year of 1951 set in, people were becoming panic-stricken. The hearsay was that the Red Chinese had entered the fray with a "human sea" strategy. In addition, the UN troops were retreating to the south, and Seoul would soon be reoccupied by the Communist Army. The chilling effect of these rumors intensified as the Siberian wind froze the air and earth of Seoul. On the second imminent occupation by the Communist forces, escape was followed by another escape, on the dark evenings of January 1951. Our family once again mixed into a stream of vagabonds, joining the mass evacuation. "We need to hurry to catch the last train," father impatiently urged us to walk faster. When we arrived at the YongDung-Po railroad station, herds of people already jammed the platform and gates. I was assigned the onerous mission of keeping an eye on the family's many bundles of possessions. I squatted myself down on one of the packs that was sitting on the platform beside the tracks. I was shivering from the cold, which was creeping allover me as I fought against drowsiness. I was so cold and tired that I lacked the ability to cry over my miserable situation. It was torture. The punishment seemed timeless.

As dawn began to overcome the night, a steam whistle announced the arrival of a freight train. As the train rolled sluggishly up to the platform, refugees began to pour onto the tracks from all directions. It was as if a cloud of ants had covered the metal beast. Every exterior inch of the train was occupied with people. There was sudden pandemonium. People were yelling and pushing to get onto the top of the freight train. Agonizing cries could be heard from those who had slipped or been pushed down, in the rush for the train. Parents and children who had become separated in what had become sheer hell, screamed for each other. Their cries made the hair on the back of my neck stand on end. By some stroke of luck, at the hands of a stranger, I was lifted onto a narrow spot on the train's head. The last exodus train started to worm its way southbound down the track. The engine hissed, and the body of the train rattled under the strain of the miserable creatures that clung to its exterior. As the train gathered speed, it let out a long, plaintive howl. A cutting north wind slashed against my frozen face. The person swinging in the small space above me passed his urine as if he were baptizing me. His lukewarm discharge quickly froze. "Damn it!! What a terrible journey!" I exploded with anger even as, notwithstanding the cold, a terrible hunger gnawed endlessly at my stomach. At times, the last freedom train blew a hollow whistle into the heavens as if expressing a lasting regret.

The winter landscape shifted quickly as the train passed. Occasionally, a wisp of smoke could be seen floating above the grass rooftops of a distant village. Knowing that these homes were cooking supper would make my stomach ache. All of the refugees were desperate for their lives as they held on to their tiny lots. The constant crying of young children was drowned out by the hissing noise of the engine. Amid this chaotic state, dreadful accidents would happen. The train sped quickly through a long, dark tunnel in a mountain. A dull *"thump"* was heard, then the shrieking voice of a woman echoed, reverberated, through the tunnel. Somebody shouted that a young woman had dropped her baby onto the train track. She had tragically loosened her hold on the baby in a moment of involuntary, drowsy, relaxation. Her wailing ensued for a long time. The freight train kept rattling away in its relentless ignorance. Sorrow shadowed another sorrow. The last exodus train carried both grief and freedom.

It was drizzling when the iron horse pulled into the harbor city of Pusan. The city is situated at the southernmost tip of Korea, facing the ocean. Countless escapees flooded into every corner of the strange land in an attempt to seek shelter. There was concern that the people of Pusan might not welcome the enormous influx of homeless people who had just invaded their city. As the winter rain grew harsher, it was by the mercy of Heaven that my father found a small room. It was a narrow, musty room. Tired to death, I fell fast asleep.

"Wake up! Wake up! We should leave tonight!" Father's rude words shook me from my deep sleep. We entered the jet-black night where sea and sky were indistinguishable from each other. The only thing I could make out were the sounds of the splashing water, and the occasional hissing of the sea wind. Suddenly, I was carried back to the pitch-dark waters of the 38th parallel. It was as if I were reliving that dark morning of March 1948. Would I ever be allowed to stay in one place? Life had become one escape after another.

I boarded the deck of a wooden ship. The sound of the boat rubbing against the wooden pier mixed with the lapping of the water against its hull. I stepped down to the dark, flat bottom of the ship. No light penetrated the interior of the vessel. As I found my way amongst the mass of writhing bodies, I was able to squeeze a space for myself between my faceless companions. We were not settled for long before the relative calm of the crowd was disturbed. By this time, my mother was in labor again. The crowd around us spontaneously moved and organized to help ensure a safe delivery. Even in these most desperate of circumstances, the kindred spirit of humanity prevailed. At last, my mother gave birth to my newest brother with the help of these kind strangers. During the tedious voyage, I enjoyed playing with the tender legs of my newborn brother who lay beside me.

The voyage seemed endless but, at last, we reached Cheju Island as the sun was setting. The well-worn ship touched shore. "Welcome! Welcome to Cheju Island!" the ROK Marines cheered, as the refugees poured onto the dock out of the ship. "Hi, kid! Let me help you!" a young Marine said, extending his warm hand to help me up the wide plank that bridged the space between the dock and the deck of the ship. Even more unexpected than the help of the Marines was the help of a number of natives who were waiting about the wharf, greeting the escapees. They heartily ushered homeless people into their own houses. We were lucky enough to be greeted by a kind, middle-aged lady. She spoke with a strongly-accented dialect and provided us with room and board. We had been successful. We had landed and had been able to fund shelter.

Our luck continued. Just days after landing on Cheju Island, father was able to find a modest cottage in a rustic village. The village was nestled at the foot of Halla Mountain. Communist guerrillas were still clinging to their mountain hideaways, but for me, a fresh new world had been unraveled. The majestic peak of Halla Mountain was crowned with white snow, while a fresh, salty breeze surrounded the entire island. The atmosphere was intoxicating, the broad leaves of the semitropical plants swayed in the sea breeze, and I fervently wished that Cheju Island would be our final refuge. I felt that this fantasy island could easily become my new home.

As we settled in, it was not long before my cousin, Chang, and I were cast into the front lines of commerce to help the household earn a living. We would dash up and down the northern shore of the island. There was a sloping hill that served as an open market. We would shout until our throats became hoarse as we roamed throughout the bustling marketplace. We called in unison: "Lucky Strike! Pall Mall! Camel! *Hwa rang Dam-bae*! ("cigarettes!")" as we hauled small wooden boxes loaded with various kinds of cigarettes around our necks. As usual, my older cousin became the senior member of the hawking business and I became his subordinate.

Every once in a while, when I was strolling by myself about the Cheju quayside, the magical seascape would capture my imagination. At these times, I would stand at the breakwater and take pleasure in watching the dark green sea roll its waves like the furling and unfurling of a straw mat. I would give my senses over to the sea, tasting the salt, feeling the cool breeze, and hearing the roaring sound of regret. At other times I would picture the surges of the sea as a living giant, while on shore was a floating time-worn Chinese ship, which appeared like a fixture. Ragged patches were hooked on its deck, fluttering in the sea wind like tattered flags of a defeated battleship. The story was that the ship's crew had lost their way while escaping from Communist China in 1948. The Chinese refugees had their destiny deeply anchored on the peaceful island of Cheju.

As springtime set in, my new life as an evacuee unfolded. I entered the Cheju North elementary school. Among the native classmates, I was like a stranger who could not completely comprehend their broad dialect. But, as the days went by, I became more acclimated to the strongly provincial nature of the island, and I could join, to some degree, my classmates at play. Every weekend I'd dash to the shore with some close native friends. We would stay from morning to dusk, stripping down to nothing and diving into the ocean, sometimes for the sheer joy of it, and sometimes to retrieve the sleek sea lettuce that was firmly attached to the rocks at the bottom of the shallow sea. When I was hungry, I'd duck under the waves and pluck the sea lettuce from the water, then spread it on the dry whinstone of the shore. Before long, the green seaweed became dry and crispy. I would then take the parched weeds and stuff them into my mouth.

At that time, I was not usually shy about being unclothed among my peers. However, I do remember one time when my naked body was witnessed by a girl of about my own age. I quickly bolted while hiding my testicles in my cupped hands. No matter what my mood was, I was able to run to the sea that embraced my soul and flesh in its boundless bosom. I would be thrilled by watching the wild waves. Sometimes I could hear the mournful tunes of the women divers as they hunted for abalone and seaweed. The women had round gourd baskets attached to them as they plunged into the raging waters. The baskets drifted on a single line as the women sought their quarry. Their song would reach my ears with a nostalgic blend of sadness and bitterness:

The bird chirping in the morning,
Cry for starvation,
Bird twittering in the evening,
Whine for missing the absent love.

While the sea was openhearted, Mount Halla was a forbidden zone. The remains of a long-fought ideological confrontation continued to smolder. Day and night, the Communist guerrillas fought against the police, sending the crackling sound of rifle-fire across the landscape. Pillars of flames frequently shot up from the heart of Mount Halla. In spite of the hatred that continued to be generated by man, the mountain itself stood aloof from the madding world. Halla Mountain was an object of wonder and fear that could not dare be accessible but to gaze at its awesome shape. Nonetheless, it was said that Halla Mountain had a history steeped in sorrow.

One cloudy afternoon, as I played at my usual spot on the shore, I happened to come across an old man who lived in a shabby cottage fenced with volcanic stones. With a half-crazed look, he would fix his blank gaze on the far horizon. Sometimes, he would wave his hands in the air as if he were appealing to something toward the sea. He was probably in his sixties, and word was that he was a survivor from the tragic uprising of April 3, 1948. A bloody conflict between the left and right wings must have made indelible scars on the people and island of Cheju. Sometimes the man would become lucid and he would mutter to himself, "I am not a Communist. I have nothing to do with Communist guerrillas. Please, don't kill our family. God damn! What the hell is with this ideology?" Soon after performing this short monologue, his face would become distorted, and he would descend into a prolonged silence. It was said that, during the April 3rd Cheju uprising, most of the islanders had been afflicted with military brutality. The old man must have had an incurable psychological trauma stemming from his experience. Whenever I stopped by to visit him at his hut, he would give me a faint smile. We would communicate silently, just by looking at each other. His eyes were always misty.

Meanwhile, there were frequent funeral processions for those who had been killed in battles with the guerrillas still hiding on Halla Mountain. The funeral train would travel down the street, and sometimes I would follow it. Once, a joint service for the war dead was held on a wide playground of North Cheju elementary school, which I attended. I joined the sad service. The atmosphere was choked by the pungent smell of incense glowing from the altar. I stared vacantly at the thin columns of blue fumes as they coiled up with the breeze toward the sky. It was as if the souls of the dead were ascending to the highest heavens, while listening to the plaintive sound of Buddhist scripture being chanted to the beat of a wooden block, helping to lift their spirits up to Paradise.

The Lord said, What have you done?
Listen! Your brother's blood cries out to me from the ground.
To kill or to be killed between brothers and brothers.
Who is Cain? Who is Abel?

The Cheju Island was a land full of tragic legends. In any case, despite its history, my life of refuge seemed to be going smoothly. But an unexpected thing happened to me: father chose me as his companion for another journey. "I don't want to leave Cheju Island," I grumbled. The involuntary trip depressed me;

however, I had no choice but to accede to his wishes. We left on a bitter evening of January of 1952. We took a ship from Cheju quay to Mock-Po Harbor. The frigid weather bit at me, adding to my discomfort and feeling of misfortune. The only thing that saved me from being frostbitten was the dogskin hat that I had wrapped around my ears and drawn over my eyes. Immediately upon our arrival, after docking at Mock-Po Harbor, we boarded a night train for Chun-An City. The train clattered on the parallel track, creating a lonesome whistle. The inside of the train was cold and dark. I whiled away the time by pressing my cheek against the dark, icy windowpane, creating a white frost with my breath. With my index finger I scraped the words: *"Who are you? Why do you stay here?"* Under the feeble lights hanging from the ceiling of the train, I shuddered in an endless, sleepless night. *"Where am I going now? Why? When will I be allowed to go back to Cheju Island?"*

While I was playing the role of soliloquist with bloodshot eyes, the day dawned.

The train pulled into the platform of Chun-An station. I caught a glimpse of a black crow crouching on the dried branch of an oak tree beside the railroad station. Caw...Caw...the bird greeted me, making a hollow echo in the dawning sky. When we came out to the street, my father waved for a ride from the passing trucks. A freight truck laden with heavy packages came screeching to a halt in front of us.

"Where are you going?" asked the driver.

"Chun-An Sam-Geu-Ri," (*"three-forked road"*) father quickly responded.

"Get in!" the driver shouted. Father picked me up and dumped me into the back of the truck. Quickly, he followed and then was beside me.

In the vicinity of Chun-An Sam-Geu-Ri, father soon opened a humble shop selling various cheap medicines. I was eight years old then and was admitted to the Chun-An elementary school, located on a hill miles from father's store. Before the first class began, a teacher introduced me to the other students. I was very nervous. My heart was beating hard and I hung my head down to my chest. As a natural introvert, I felt awkward and shy in this new environment. Every morning before the first class commenced, the school playground would be congested with children playing soccer, a ball game that was very popular with them. I would walk around the playground by myself, watching the other children run back and forth, filling the air with clouds of yellow dust. In addition to my school life, I was drawn to church every Sunday by the bells of the Chun-An Methodist church. The red bricks of the church towered above the hill, making an impressive stance above the city. The Sunday school replenished me with spiritual food as much as play replenished my body.

On a bright morning in late October of 1952, our Sunday school went for an excursion into the countryside. Along the footpath and amidst the golden sea of a rippling rice paddy in the autumn breeze, I came across many of nature's wonders – the melodious sound of babbling water in the ditch among the rice fields, the small silver carp bouncing up over the sparkling stream under the crisp autumn sunlight, the ceaseless chirping of a flock of sparrows coveting the well-ripened grain, and lastly, the abundant grasshoppers popping in and out among the dense stems of rice. In nature's garden, the Sunday school teacher implanted a strong impression in our young minds. The story of Abraham Lincoln's childhood and how he had been raised in poverty, yet to become the President of the United

States, impressed us. This gave us a sense of hope.

Meanwhile, the world of man, different from the natural world, kept going to the devil. Radio broadcasts continued to report the advancement and retreat in the battles taking place at the nearby 38th parallel. Every corner of Chun-An City showed signs of the ravages of war. Young orphans in rags begged from door to door with empty cans tied around their necks. Wounded soldiers wandered aimlessly on the streets and widows were found squatting at every corner, selling rice cakes. It seemed that every day brought more scenes of sadness. The war must have created a myriad of sorrowful stories. In the meantime, yet another change was to burst abruptly into my life.

One day in late December of 1952, for reasons unknown to me, my father closed his shop. It seemed that, just as abruptly as we had come, we were leaving again. "Let's go back to Cheju Island, and on the way, we should stop to see your grandfather." I boarded the morning train headed for the rural district of Seu-Chun. Seated next to a window, I engaged in a peculiar daydream throughout the entire trip. It seemed so realistic that I had a hard time distinguishing the two.

Grandfather lived alone, secluded from the rest of the world. Since his escape from the north, he had confined himself from the outside world as an ascetic priest. Immediately after the Japanese imperialistic wind had receded, the Communist storm from Siberia had swept into the northern parts of Korea. In a single day, my grandfather had been reduced to a pauper. A deadly monster called ideology had disintegrated his entire life.

"Welcome! Welcome!" he greeted me, with a faint smile on his face, letting his long beard stream in the breeze. "You know, the division of this country will be prolonged. It may be permanent. I am too old, and it is hopeless to think that I could return to my hometown. I am thinking, this place is my final resting place. But it is different for you, because you are young. As you know, I worked hard all my life, not only for my family but for the service of the church. I prayed to God for the independence of the fatherland from the brutal Japanese control. It all came to nothing. My dream was broken to pieces. I have come to the realization that this world is nothing but an illusion. Do not make strong attachments to anything of this world. Suffering will never cease, particularly, on this Korean peninsula. Get away, as far as you can. My time is coming to an end, but you do not have to share in my fate."

He made this speech as if it were to be his last. It seemed to me that, as he poured out his life's regrets, he only wished that his past could be wiped into oblivion.

Grandfather's hermitage was enclosed by a bamboo thicket with pheasants flying in and out. Periodically, in order to make a living, my grandfather would go to the open market that was held once a week and was only a few miles from his home. One snowy morning, three generations of Kims set out to peddle at the market. Father carried a pack of bamboo articles on his back. The three of us set out along the snow-laden mountain path that followed the frozen Seu-Chun Lake. We trudged along in silence down the snow-covered, bumpy road. I was trailing a step behind the two men. It was a land of desolation, and the homogeneous, white-colored sky and earth narrowed my vision. Now and then the rhythmical sound of the snow creaking under the boots of the three of us, provoked a strange sensation. My small toes throbbed with blisters. The mountain path to survival seemed too far away. The three refugees, each representing his own generation, spent the entire winter season together, as in a legend in the sacred land far away from the lunacy of war.

Yellow Dahlias Among the Ruins

In the spring of 1953, when the frozen land began to thaw, my father and I returned to Cheju Island. The summit of Halla Mountain, capped with its white snow, was shining with the reflection of the sun. In spite of the fine scenery of Cheju Island, things had changed. There seemed to be a cloud of gloom hanging over the whole island. The radio broadcasted that the war was still in the balance at the 38th parallel. Every morning, US heavy trucks packed with POWs – Communist soldiers – came and went on the dusty street in front of our house. Grandmother would poke her head out the window, hoping to see her youngest son among the faces. However, without fail, her dream would not come true. Even though she had been given notice that her son was dead, she never gave up hope that he would return. His homecoming became her sole purpose. "My son will come back. There is no reason that he should die before me. I know he will come back..."

The armistice talks dragged on without any sign of progress, but finally, on July 27, 1953, an agreement was signed. The treaty drew a line of demarcation at the 38th parallel of Korea, dividing the country. The North Communist Army and the UN forces had suffered combined casualties exceeding four million people. The 38th line became even more solidified than it had been before the war. Dreams of going back to one's hometown and being reunited with family members were shattered. Refugees began to desert Cheju Island. "Let's go back to Seoul. There is no reason for us to stay here now that the war is suspended. There is no way to know how long the division of the country will last. For three years now, war has made this country nothing but a human slaughterhouse, and nobody will take responsibility for the catastrophe that has become the Korean peninsula." Father railed with deep bitterness and released a long sigh. "If God is righteous in his existence, why does he continue to inflict such misery on the Korean people, who have never inflicted any ill will on any of their neighboring countries. It is senseless. Is this so-called ideology worth the killing of millions of innocent people? Of course not. This has all been so irrational."

With equal amounts of delight and misgiving, we returned to the capital city, Seoul. After three years of living life on the run, we were looking forward to some stability. However, the Seoul we returned to was much different than the one we had left. The railroad station was stirring with crowds of people, but the city itself was a skeleton of its former self. Countless buildings had been destroyed, and the town of Tapgol¬Seung-Bang was shadowed by Seoul's spiritless gloom. The courtyard of our house was overgrown with huge, dark weeds. The brick roof was spotted with the growth of coarse plants. The interior rooms showed unmistakable signs of fervent rodent activity and smelled of decay. Ironically, the innermost recess of the courtyard was home to a bunch of yellow dahlias that was shining joyfully and nodding in the faint breeze. Young orphans knocked on every door for food. Disabled soldiers who had been discharged from the army cried out incoherently, and were known to sometimes swing their crutches at people.

The war had taken everything from these people, including their dignity. The rudeness of the wounded soldiers was beyond description. Nobody had the audacity to stand up against their arrogance. Even the police were reluctant to become involved in the public commotion they created. They harassed their fellow citizens, obviously considering themselves to be of a privileged class. One day, a band of disabled veterans, clothed in discolored green uniforms, broke into my father's shop. Their imposing bodies filled the space. One of them attempted to blackmail my father. He waved his hand about and said, "You know who we are! We need your help!"

At first, my father responded in a polite but firm voice. "I fully understand your situation. As you know, I can scarcely make a living for my family. I am able to donate a little. I know that this amount is not enough for you, but it is all that I am able to spare. I hope that you understand my difficult circumstances, as I understand yours." As father concluded his speech, their attitude changed abruptly.

Their faces became menacing, and they threw the paper money that father had offered them onto the floor. They rained a shower of verbal abuses on us and lifted their crutches in a threatening manner. "You bastard! You think we are beggars, you son of a bitch! We sacrificed for you! God damn you!" The shop became a scene of wreckage. It did not take father long to recover his wits and counter their attack.

"You shut up!" he yelled. "I am a fellow veteran, discharged due to my war wounds. My little brother was killed on the front line. We have all suffered from this war. We have all lost family and friends. We are all victims of the war, not just you! You are lucky to be alive. Do you understand? If you continue to insult and threaten me I will break your necks!" Father glared at them while raising his voice. The men shrewdly withdrew themselves from the shop.

Similar incidents played themselves out on a regular basis. Father became accustomed to the role of defender, as there was no other way but to strike back against their antagonistic advances. "There are so many disabled soldiers that we can't control them," said the policemen. "They have nothing but their own kind of sad desperation. In the post-war days, people had a very pessimistic outlook. We are living in a time bomb, and sooner or later another war will come along. Who knows, one atomic bomb and our whole nation may be obliterated. Who will be the victor and who will be defeated?"

In addition to the legacy of poverty and discontent, the war produced an awful famine. It was not uncommon to go hungry. My elementary school sporadically provided children with foreign-aid goods. The best days were when small amounts of powdered milk were distributed. I would fill a small can with the powdered milk and heat the can in a pot of boiling water. After a few minutes, the dry milk would turn into a stony, yellowish bar. I would then let pieces of the milk bar melt in my mouth, while the sweet flavor trickled down my throat. On the days when we were lucky enough to get the milk bars, our sole treat at that time, the poverty and misery of the war were temporarily abated.

On the days when depression did overtake me, I was

spontaneously drawn to the serenity of the Buddhist temple. As before the war, the precincts of the temple seemed to sublimate me into an ethereal world. Despite three years of brutal war, the Buddhist statues remained intact, with no bullet marks. Many devotees who had suffered in the war came in flocks to worship before the image of the golden Buddha, who perched cockily at the center of the high altar. He continued to smile with half-closed eyes, as if he were sneering. Despite Buddha's ironic expression, more people thronged to the temple than before the war. While the Buddhist priests chanted scripture, a train of widowed women offered a Buddhist service. With their tearful faces, these women who had lost their husbands or sons, burned their sorrows as they burned their incense, wishing their beloved ones to be reincarnated. The doleful scenes of the temple hypnotized me, creating a sense of wretchedness mingled with an inscrutable beauty. The surroundings of the church that I attended every Sunday morning were much brighter than the sad mood of the Buddhist temple. Nevertheless, the shadow of the temple seemed to be quite compatible with the light of the church, neither detracting from the other.

The Death of a Little Angel

The spring of 1956 marked the end of my early childhood that had been interspersed with war and flight. The change was punctuated by my departure from the village of Tapgol-Seung-Bang, which had been my base since our escape from the north in 1948. I found myself settling down in a strange town close to Chung-Ryang railroad station. In contrast with my boyhood, my early teens brought a more distinct consciousness than the hazy sense of my dreamy childhood. The clear awareness was bound to bring about more agony than the dim vision of infancy.

In March of 1956, I was admitted to a mission school and simultaneously enrolled as a member of a Sunday school in a Presbyterian church that was erected on a sloping hillside of the neighboring, low mountain. That same year, on Christmas Eve, all the members of the Sunday school Bible class gathered at the house of the president of the student council to rehearse carol songs. Fifteen young teens, boys and girls, were crowded into a small room. I was the youngest among them. At first, I was nervous to be around girls. However, the friendly atmosphere soon quelled my misgivings. We all sang our songs with fervor and enjoyed pleasant intervals between sets.

The church had scheduled us to carol from midnight until dawn. As midnight drew closer, we split into two teams. The leader of my team was a girl named Miock. She had a fair complexion and a shape that left an agreeable impression. It was believed that Christmas Eve was darker than other nights. My team plunged into the frozen field, braving the arctic wind. In spite of the freezing weather, the thought of accompanying Miock filled me with a rather warm sense of ecstasy.

Silent night, holy night, all is calm, all is bright.
'Round yon Virgin Mother and child,
Holy infant so tender and mild,
Sleep in heavenly peace. Sleep in heavenly peace.

We sang the song in chorus as a regular carol among several other songs. It was hard to sing through the chattering of my teeth. However, the frigid temperature did have a welcome side effect. We all huddled together for warmth, and found ourselves hand in hand. In the darkness, Miock whispered to me in a subdued voice, as if she were my older sister, "Young! You look cold. It is a cold night." All the while, she clasped my cold hand in the warmth of her own. Her natural smell was that of wild, sweet flowers, and it instantly threw me into a sense of mysterious euphoria. After our special meeting on that Christmas Eve, I looked forward to Sunday school and the chance to see Miock's face. When I did see her, I would shrink away in shyness. The passion for her was burning up in secret at the core of my heart like a little bonfire, partly in tantalization, partly in happiness. How can I forget the first touch of her slim hand?

Our teacher had been widowed in the war and often had

fits of weeping while she was praying. "Oh! My love Jesus! Oh! My love Jesus!" she repeated over and over again, verging on hysteria. The students would sit in stunned silence. It occurred to me that her praying was a kind of elegy for her beloved husband. Instead of calling out to him, she cried, "Oh! My love Jesus!"

Bitterly she weeps at night, tears are upon her cheeks,
Among all her lovers, there is none to comfort her.
(Lamentations: 1 :2)

My friendship with Miock matured as the weeks progressed. She greeted me every Sunday morning without fail. Her gentle voice reached my ears like a gospel angel. "Young, how are you?" she would ask.

I would stammer in reply, "Um...I...'m...okay." Sometimes, Miock would turn up in my dreams. We would be walking hand in hand across a desolate field under a starlit sky. The romantic dream would sadly end with the two of us separating at a fork, one of us going north, the other south.

I somehow became aware of her family's history. Her father had been a prominent professor at the Kyeung-Sung Imperial University when Japan had control over the Korean peninsula. Her mother was a modem woman who had graduated with a major in fine arts. With the approach to an end of the Japanese rule over Korea, Communist dogma permeated the public. It particularly infiltrated the minds of many of the intellectuals, which included many professors and young students, like an epidemic. As the country became liberated, the Communist ideology became more inflamed.

One day, Miock's parents had a heated argument. Her

father insisted that they go north, where Communism had already taken hold. Her mother was a very religious person and insisted that they stay in the south. It was a crucial division of ideas, one on which life and death were staked. The parents had argued all night without reaching an agreement. A few months before the war broke out, they parted ways. Miock's father left, alone, to go to the north. Her mother remained with her three young children in the south.

The new, monstrous ideology begot the division not only of the Korean peninsula but also of Miock's family and many other families as well. The division pushed Miock's family onto a dark path. Even though Miock's mother was a pious Christian who served the church leader in evangelical work, the police put her family on the blacklist due to her husband's history. To make things worse, she was unable to make a living. Miock's family story broke my heart.

One Sunday morning I noticed that Miock was looking very pale. "Miock, you look tired," I said. "Are you okay?"

"Yes, I'm fine," she answered, staring vacantly at me and pausing to smile.

In the ruins of war, many homeless people lived wherever they could find space to lie down. Miock's family had built a wretched nest in a deserted, skeletal building that had been bombed during the war. The roof had been torn off. A couple of makeshift tattered curtains, made from rice straw were attached to a torn straw mat that lay on the bare soil. This was all the family had to shelter themselves from the natural elements. There was no heat and no hot water. Miock was in a desperate situation and was vulnerable to any diseases that came along. As time went by, Miock's health continued to deteriorate. Despite her bitter life, she never complained about anything.

Instead, her innocent smile evoked a sense of sorrow.

In December of 1957, on a windy Sunday morning, Miock called me aside before Bible class began. "Young," she said, "I would like you to keep this Bible. From now, it is yours." She spoke as though she were talking to a younger brother.

"Why do you want to give me your Bible?" I asked. I was worried and perplexed. At the bottom of the first page she had written one simple sentence: "To Young Kim, from Miock." I treasured her gift as if it were her incarnation. However, I had a premonition that misfortune was looming.

As Christmas Day of 1957 drew near, I hoped to have another Christmas carol encounter with Miock. But her health seemed to get worse on a daily basis. She was conspicuously feeble. One Sunday she did not make it to Sunday school. I was instantly filled with an overwhelming feeling of dread. I became mesmerized by the dried branches of the big acacia tree as they were blown about in a howling winter storm. As afternoon approached, a blizzard of snowflakes began to whirl. The Bible teacher suggested that we visit Miock at her sickbed. Several of us instantly accepted her offer. As we walked out of the church, we saw that the world was blanketed in white. In some ways, the snowcap intensified my feeling of horror.

Miock was lying on a damp straw mat, her eyes closed. There was no heat. Her mother, who was nursing her, seemed confused by our sudden visit. I was shocked at Miock's bloodless face. The Bible teacher grasped Miock's hand and called her name in a soothing voice. Miock remained motionless. The Bible teacher started to pray. Her voice quivered and she had a lump in her throat. The hollow sound of water, dripping from somewhere above, intensified the feeling of hopelessness. "My love Jesus. My love Jesus. Please help my dear student,

Miock, recover her health quickly." She prolonged the prayer by repeating the term, "My love Jesus," as though she were chanting a spell. "My love Jesus, please relieve Miock from her suffering." Every student kneeled down beside the straw bed. After a while, Miock barely opened her eyes and smiled vaguely at us. We exchanged glances.

Three days later, the teacher gave us the awful news. In a trembling voice and with a tear-stained face, she said, "Dear students, our beloved Miock passed away early this morning. The doctor said she died of acute pneumonia and malnutrition." The news overwhelmed us, as if we were drowning in a sea of sorrow. I became numb. Out of nowhere, an image struck me. She was not only a little blue magpie that had brought me a supreme happiness, even if only for a short time, but she was also a cuckoo that left a profound and everlasting sorrow on my heart. The acacia tree outside the window was shaking convulsively in the high wind.

Once, after Miock died, she showed up in my dream. "Young," she said, "come over here. Why are you over there? Come here." I tried to touch her hand, in vain. To me, Miock was a little angel who became a martyr in the divided time of the tragic Korean history. Miock's departure from this world left me without motivation to go to church. The Bible teacher's praying had been nothing more than an empty reverberation. Christmas Eve is a constant reminder to me of Miock's death. She is a lonesome star among a myriad of others in the cold, dark heavens. I must have loved a little angel on this earth. With the death of Miock, my early puberty passed away with deep remorse.

The Cry of the Gods

The formal religious teachings that I received from the mission school differed greatly from my earlier experience with religion; they were an artificial pressure that was totally different from the spontaneous encounters I had experienced in my early childhood. Bible class was now a compulsory subject: no Bible study credits, no graduation. In a religious foundry, all students had to have their natural dispositions cast into a spiritually identical quality. The school infused Christian doctrines into the naive lambs' minds and intimidated the students with stories about how those who did not believe in God under the name of Jehovah would be cursed from generation to generation, suffering eternal flames. If one followed their dogma, I wondered, what would become of my atheist grandfather, and my grandmother who followed a mixture of Buddhism and traditional Korean shamanism. I wondered what may have become of my youngest uncle, who was killed during the Korean War but was not a Christian. I wondered about my father, who refused to belong to any religious organization, in an attempt not to be swayed by any human ideological persuasions. And last, I wondered about all the countless innocent people, Korean or otherwise, who had died before Jehovah was introduced to them. Were they all condemned to hell? It appeared to me that the Bible could be contradictory in nature. On the one hand, it was filled with sophisticated ideas, but on the other hand, it demanded blind obedience.

In spite of my problems with parts of the Bible, the book touched my heart in a very meaningful way. Among the mountains of words in the Bible, the word of Jesus, written down in John 10:34-35, rang true to me as the ultimate gospel:

Is it not written in your Law,
"I have said you are gods"?
If he called them "gods," to whom the word of God came—
and the scripture cannot be broken—

I thought that the so-called God did not have a privileged existence, was not more than a human being, and not less than a man; rather, that he had a universal mind and a warm-hearted touch.

In spite of the holy teaching, the reality was unfavorable for the weak. The lofty ideals were often hollow words. I had a bosom friend who was poverty-stricken. At every lunchtime meal, his classmates made a united effort to help him. One of his friends provided him with room and board. This meant that the two of them had to share a very cramped living space. On the other hand, the school was pitiless in regard to his situation.

One morning, before class began, the teacher in charge made my friend stand up. "What happened to your tuition? It is past due!" the teacher, who considered himself very religious, yelled at my friend in front of the rest of the class. My friend looked calm despite the indignity that had been heaped upon him. He had become accustomed to being humiliated by his teacher. Though he came of a poor family, I never heard that he ever complained about his distressing circumstances. When the weather was nice, he used to paint in a shady corner of the school playground. I would watch him bring his dreams to life with his skilled use of watercolor. It seemed to me, from the point of view of a student, that we young students were more pure and humanitarian to the needs of our companions than the hypocritical adults.

Our school soccer team fell victim to what seemed to be an arbitrary rule. Our team had won all of its games. The final countrywide competition was scheduled on a Sunday. The team was told that it would not be allowed to play in this decisive contest, due to the mission school's regulations prohibiting any form of activity on Sundays. Despite the school's opposition, the players participated in the finals. To make matters worse, the students flocked to the field to encourage their team. The day after the game, the entire team was subjected to disciplinary action; they were suspended from school for some time. I could not help but wonder if the religious dogmas were so important that they should be used to obliterate the pure joy and willfulness of young teenagers. The school's decision seemed to be ridiculous.

God chose the lowly things of this world
And the despised things – (Corinthians 1. 28)

I interpreted the passage to mean that God might be among the common things of life, instead of among the chosen specialties of religious dogma, and that Jesus might be one among a myriad of common beings in the world.

The golden bells on the hills of the campus heralded the beginning of spring 1960. The brilliant colors of the spring days were in complete contrast with the oppressively heavy atmosphere hanging over the campus. The feeling of discontent was even more intensely felt throughout the country. People were panic-stricken by the tyranny of the government; gangsters who conspired with the politicians kept harassing citizens. The police brutally arrested innocent people without a warrant. Anyone who complained about the harsh treatment was branded a "communist" and tortured to death under the guise of "anti-communist control." Resentment of the government seemed to be coming to a boiling point. The populace had suspicions about the fact that many of the high-ranking government officials, including President Lee Seung Man, were devout Christians. In addition to that, many policemen holding high-ranking positions were pro-Japanese and had been agents who had tortured and killed their fellow Koreans under the cruel Japanese occupation. President Lee and his corrupt regime worried that their government might collapse.

Consequently, on general election day, March 15, 1960, Lee's government staged an illegal election, mobilizing the police and their gangsters throughout the nation. Making things worse was a report in the American press that a fisherman in Ma-San City, located in the southern part of Korea, reeled in a high school student named Kim Ju Yeul. It had been determined that Kim Ju Yeul had been brutally killed and thrown into the sea by the police. This tragic news ignited the frustration that had been smoldering deep in the hearts of many ordinary people. A burning rage began to spread uncontrollably through the nation. Ultimately, the capital city of Seoul was enveloped in rage. The flames of discontent were further fueled by a cruel attack on students by terrorists supported by Lee's government. Many students, who had been staging a peaceful demonstration in the street, were attacked and killed. Consequently, on April 19th, 1960, a cataclysmic event took place.

It was a bright spring morning, but the atmospheric mood hovered heavily over our campus. At the very moment the first bell rang for classes to begin, urgent cries were heard from all directions: "Let's go!" "Get out of here!" "Come on, everybody!" "Hurry up!" On hearing their fellow students' outcries, the rest of the student body spontaneously sprang up as if they had been waiting for this moment. Without hesitation, the young students rushed to the fence surrounding the campus. The teachers doggedly tried to prevent their students from advancing. They feared that the police or gangsters would hurt the students. But everything was happening too quickly. It was pointless to try to stop the students, for it seemed to be God's will. Jumping over the concrete fence, the students ran toward the National Assembly Building. We formed a scrimmage line, but before we could make much progress, we encountered an obstacle. Armed policemen met us in the middle of the road and began to beat us indiscriminately. With the pandemonium and merciless onslaught, our line quickly collapsed. Having run out of the school with no plan in mind, we were lost immediately in a tactical breakdown. After quickly regrouping, we headed in another direction but were blocked again by other policemen. We had no choice but to limp back to the school.

Yet, something ominous was brewing. It was not long before we were called to the schoolyard. A school chaplain climbed on top of a platform. "Dear students!" he said. "Our school has decided to join in the demonstration against the illegal election committed by the present regime! Dear students, before reentering the streets, let us pray to our God!" The students wore the tense faces of soldiers ready for battle, and the pastor's voice quivered with his tears. His prayer touched the students' hearts and filled their souls with tragic resolution.

By early afternoon the students and teachers had left the school together in resolute columns. "Down with the illegal election! Down with LeeSeung Man!!" The teachers and their students screamed with one voice in the chaotic streets. Hordes of people gathered in the wide-open square of the Capital City Building. In the middle of the square, some young people got on their trucks and frantically waved their blood-soaked shirts. Their battle cries were punctuated by the successive gunshots that could be heard ringing out in the vicinity. It is said that the police began to shoot indiscriminately at the students who were gathered in front of the President's Residence. There were hundreds of casualties. God's children were bleeding for their righteous cause. The revolution must have needed the bloodshed of the innocent.

As dusk gathered, the people retreated and dispersed to their own locations. As I trudged along the main road that led to my house a few miles out of downtown, I was struck with the desolation of the streets. It was as if a whirlwind had passed through and disrupted everything. Police boxes were burned down or had shattered windowpanes. Voluminous black smoke rose from the main police station and trailed into the blood-red evening sky. Everything seemed to be in a state of anarchy. Not a single policeman was to be seen. All the way home, the dismal sight of the deserted streets filled my heart with terror.

On April 20, 1960, the day after the students' uprising, President Lee, with a trembling voice, broadcasted his resignation. The students had defeated the seemingly undefeatable dictatorship. Lee Ki-Bung, the President's second-in-command, felt that he had no choice but to eradicate his family in order to spare them further shame. First, the eldest son shot his parents dead. Secondly, he fired a shot at his younger brother, and lastly he killed himself. Yet, the man who was truly responsible for all of the tragic occurrences, President Lee Seung Man, snuck out of the country the day after his resignation. Just as he had fled Seoul during the war in 1950, he played the coward's role again. What a poor old man he was. He must have been born a traitor to his dear people.

The student revolution ended in both elation and in sorrow. Many innocent students had died. Yet, I am very proud to have been an eyewitness to the historical events of the April revolution. The bloody scene of that crucial day will always be fossilized in the recesses of my memory. As always, the events of man were mocked by nature. Even with all the happiness and sadness of that fateful month, the hill of my school was ablaze with a blooming band of yellow forsythias. The unruly blooms beamed at the warriors of the revolution, as if nothing had happened.

At the Crossroads of Confusion

At dawn on May 16, 1961, about a year after the student revolution, gunshot awakened the Seoulites. An urgent voice on the radio announced that a military revolution had come into effect. As the day broke, the capital city, Seoul was already under the occupation forces. Heavily-armed military men were dispersed throughout the city. Many tanks were posted on street corners. This unforeseen sight stunned me.

My father, however, was offended. "Damn! All those hundreds of young souls, dying for a revolution, for an ideal, and these men just come in and take over? What was the point of their sacrifice if the military can just come in and wipe everything away? This is a military *coup d'etat*, not a revolution! Under their deceptive pretext they have robbed this country! Their action is illegal and cannot be justified! How can they overthrow a democratic government that was established at the cost of the students' lives? They are deceiving us now. Mark my words: in the days to come, they will drive the people of this country with a reign of terror. Damn! Damn it! This country has seen too many vermin.

"The alien ideologies literally created a division in this

country," he continued, ranting. "The partition was born of war and the conflict bred a dictatorship and a mountain of sorrows. The autocracy brought a revolution, which resulted in another military insurgency. Korean people are not lucky. This may be an irony of history. Ever since the Three Kingdoms of Korea were inappropriately merged by the Silla Kingdom which conspired with Tang forces of China in 668 AD, the withered Korean peninsula has fallen prey to vermin from both natives and foreigners. Can it be determined who has brought this endless tragedy to the Koreans? Korea is still filled with that kind of vermin. The rebel troops are also rats that will annoy the people as we go forward. I think there is no hope for this country."

I kept listening to his long monologue. Finally, he spoke as if he had made up his mind. Just to let me know how serious he was, he said, "Let's leave this country. We need to get out. You know what I mean?"

"Do you mean, to become refugees again?" I asked, in a discouraged tone.

"You are right. This time will be the last," he said.

He probably had no choice but to cling to this idea of escape to another country. He seemed to slip more and more into uneasiness, day after day. He became increasingly attached to his idea of emigrating. Every day I became more nervous. One day he would talk optimistically about the future, the next he would drop into a pessimistic pit. Hope and despair were intertwined. Sometimes, he liked to talk about the historian, H.G. Wells, who had a skeptical view of the human future. Even though he was not a Christian, he believed in the eschatology of Christianity. "You know," my father would announce negatively, "this world is going to the dogs sooner or later." Then I figured that father was not only an idealist but also a nihilist. In many ways, I understood my father and felt for him. However, on rare occasions, I became tired of his departure from the realities of everyday life. On those occasions, I would revolt against him: "You are only an idealist. Eventually, idealists are going to be extinct." I would speak rudely to him, but then I would soon repent of my impudent attack on his defeated mind. Yet he seemed to care nothing for my impolite remarks. As I kept insisting that today was more important than tomorrow, he would maintain that the future was more important than the present. His sense of reality took a toll on him. His idealistic visions could not get him through daily life. Slowly, his anxieties would transfer to me without my knowledge.

By this time, the "insurgent army" had proclaimed martial law throughout the country. The military declared public pledges of six articles. In the last clause of their provisions, they promised to return to their original military duties immediately after the completion of their stipulations.

"They are liars," my father said. "They will never give up their power. You wait and see. I lost everything in the north. I no longer have an attachment to either the north or the south. I could build another fortune in the south, only to have it all taken away from me again. I could even lose my life. We have suffered a lot since crossing the 38th parallel. In order to survive, I think we must leave. Unification? We don't know when it might come. It may not come in my generation, or in yours. It may not even come in your children's generation."

As usual, my father rambled on. Finally, I interrupted, "I agree with you, father. We should leave Korea." For the first time in many days, father broke into a broad smile.

"This challenge may be the last time we have to be refugees," he added. From the moment I echoed my father's ideas, I became a follower of his idealism.

That year, in the late spring, my mother brought surprising news from church. An elder of the church that my mother attended was accepting applications for agricultural immigration to Brazil. The news grabbed our attention. Father applied without hesitation. Meanwhile, since my school was closed for summer vacation, I volunteered at the peasant's academy. The school was located on the outskirts of Seoul. A pious Christian who was a refugee from the north had established the school. It was early afternoon when I arrived at the academy. As I entered, I saw an old man with a dignified face, strolling near the farm. "Good afternoon, sir," I said, and made a polite bow to him, ninety degrees, with my head down toward the ground.

"Welcome, student," he answered, glaring at me for a moment before he turned his white-haired head back to his business. Walking into the farmland, the strong smell of cow manure assaulted me. There were a number of idle cows, as well as young, white lambs jumping about a vast green field. Bees buzzed with their acrobatic flight in the empty air. I stepped into one of the unrefined, one-story buildings which, like military barracks, contrasted starkly with the peaceful rustic surroundings.

However, these barracks perfectly suited the ensuing training courses, which were run as strictly as on any army base. We started at 6:00 a.m. when the morning reveille was clanged and went on until the last toll at 10:00 p.m. During daylight hours, students were intensively drilled on farming methods. In the late evening, the elder, Mr. Kim, tried to infuse the Christian spirit into the minds of his students. Occasionally he would let us vehemently sing various hymns, as if we were valiantly singing military songs. To me, he conjured the image of the great friar, St. Francis. Mr. Kim was the first spiritual mentor who awakened in me the divinity of nature and its labors. I imagined that if I got the chance to go to Brazil, I would have a farm that was as idyllic and idealistic as his.

When the last bell struck, we were to turn off all the lights. The students burrowed their bodies into the dark green mattresses that were laid down side by side. I had a hard time getting to sleep. The moonlight would invade stealthily through the window, and a chorus of boisterous frogs would deafen my ears. All sorts of thoughts ran through my mind. The exquisite contrast between the serene moonlight and the desperate clamor of frogs drove me into a sentimental reverie that let me cruise aimlessly on a wide ocean of imagination. This journey of delusion seemed endless.

When I came home, father told me that the project for Brazil had fallen through. He was obviously disappointed but tried to put on a brave face: "Don't worry; we will wait for another chance." It appeared to me that my father's plans to leave the country were not going to go as smoothly as we had hoped. I instantly regretted not having spent my summer studying. It was time for high school seniors to apply to colleges and I had not prepared at all. Even though I had not studied for the entrance examination, I applied to a university. Not surprisingly, I was not selected. As a last resort I submitted another application to a second-level college. As luck would have it, there were not many applicants for the subject I chose, and I was admitted.

The very air of the college smelled of a Buddhist scent that was totally different from that of the mission school I had previously attended. In my first class, a Buddhist professor, Mr. Hong, scribbled off an ancient Zen poem in Chinese characters on the blackboard:

Life is the same as a segment of cloud rises up.
Death is also like the vanishing of a fragment of cloud.
The drifting cloud has no essential substance.
Both the life and the death are as one.

The professor reeled off the Buddhist scriptures, explaining that Buddhism is not a religion, but a philosophy, that life and death are just cycles of nature, that death is never a tragedy but rather, natural. Everybody has equal origins in the nature of Buddha. One can only attain divine enlightenment by searching for the truth in one's mind, not in outside forces. The Zen poem instantly reminded me of a passage from Genesis:

For dust you are and to dust you will return.

I thought Christianity was in many ways homogeneous with Buddhism. But mostly, since the dream of going to Brazil had collapsed, I was at a crossroads of spiritual confusion, and college life held little interest for me.

At about that time a classmate, named Jun-il, befriended me and became my savior. He was kind, with long hippie hair, and an artistic talent. "Hey, Young," he said one day, "why don't you come to my house sometime?" We became instant friends. We walked to his house together every day after school. He lived in a board-framed dingy hut that was patched with cloth. It was in the red-light district, and his neighborhood was teeming with whores. When we entered the narrow, dusty road on which my friend resided, the prostitutes were delighted to see him and treated him like a brother. They would greet him with soothing voices. As we walked through his part of town, I noticed strange men leaving the area. They were clearly there for some kind of dealings with these prostitutes. If any man walked by without acknowledging these women, he would be relentlessly insulted. But they were kind to my friend Jun-il because he was part of their town. They were extremely kind to their neighbors, and it seemed they wished to keep as much human dignity as they could.

My friend's place had two small rooms that faced each other, and a narrow space between the two rooms that was used as a kitchen and storage room. Day after day, I hung around with my friend in his somber room. His room was so dark that even a patch of sunlight could not penetrate. Strangely, the gloomy atmosphere never dampened my spirits. On the contrary, his stuffy, dull room gave me a sense of peace. It was like a refuge that calmed my roving thoughts. It was the only place where I could be free from the pressures of life. We would talk long into the night, drinking rice wine and chain-smoking cigarettes. Jun-il lived with his widowed mother. His father had died during the war, before Jun-il was born. Since widowed, she made home-brewed rice wine for a living. She treated me as if I were her second son. At every meal, she brought to the table food for two sons. I felt cozier there than I did in my own house. She was another unfortunate victim of the division of Korea. Jun-il said that his mother was widowed less than a year after she had married his father. Jun-il's talk used to excite me a great deal. He took a strong interest in both art and farming but, in practice, he was an artist. A small-sized oil painting of farmland hung on the wall of his room. "Young, listen," he said. "I have a dream to be a farmer in the future. We should share this dream together. This is not an escape from reality or hard work. I like a challenge." He seemed full of simple dreams.

On one particular day, one of Jun-il's friends Chang-

Shik dropped by. He was a woodblock artist who had won a prestigious prize at the National Art Exhibit. He and I soon became friends as well. He was tall and pure of heart. Late in November of 1962, while we were sitting around drinking rice wine, Jun-il proposed a plan: "I have an idea. Christmas is right around the corner. If we make custom Christmas cards, we could make a fortune! What do you think? Let's start right now!" He was so inspired by his idea that the three of us agreed to it in an instant. Elated by Jun-il's brainstorm, we hunkered down in the narrow den to put the project into action. Chang-Shik engraved wooden planks with different designs, and Jun-il and I followed his instructions. "Look at this picture. Beautiful, isn't it?" Chang-Shik shouted joyfully. "Beautiful! Nice card!" Jul-il and I joined him with approval. I admired his artwork with a deep sigh. I was more than a little optimistic with the expectation that the cards might sell well, due to the fact that I was in dire straits. We each carried a heavy sack filled with Christmas cards and distributed the cards on consignment to retail stationery shops in downtown Seoul City.

On our way home, we stopped in a shabby Chinese restaurant to warm our frozen bodies. Two bottles of Chinese hard liquor and a dish of crispy fried dumplings were ordered. Intoxicated by the strong wine, we began to talk a mockery of philosophy. Jun-il opened his heart first with an inarticulate speech:

"Hey! As you know, I live in the same gutter that many street girls are swarming in. What do you think of my dear sisters? Most of them are war orphans or poverty-stricken. Let's be frank. Do you think they are garbage people? As far as I know, they are not crooked; they are not hypocrites. Though my sisters sell their bodies, they never sell their spirits. Even among the ancestors of Jesus, there was a prostitute named Rahab, and Mary Magdalene. Nearly everybody, including his closest disciples, betrayed Jesus. But the prostitute, Mary Magdalene, never broke her faith in Jesus. Siddhartha was the same. When he completed his long and ascetic practice of six years, the first person who provided him with food was a street girl. We must rid ourselves of the scum of prejudice. A bias is the most malevolent of all traps. We get caught up in all kinds of distorted views; in particular, the ideological partiality between the south and the north is the worst case."

Jun-il boiled over with crazy talk, especially in vindication of his street sisters. Then, Chang-Shik started in on his own brand of philosophy: "What about the crazy artists, Van Gogh and Gauguin? I think these two men were saddened by the corruption of the world. I think art is really a religion, isn't it? These two artists were great founders of their own faith." Chang-Shik warmed up to his subject.

"Okay, okay, both of you are right," I interrupted, telling myself that they were talking crazily. "A toast! A toast! For our dear sisters and the great, crazy artists!"

The day after Christmas, we toured the shops where we had consigned the cards.

We were hoping to collect a lot of money; however, our first entrepreneurial venture did not turn out as planned. Nevertheless, we were not discouraged. We took the meager amount of money we had made and immediately went back to the same Chinese restaurant. We three crazy youngsters had a wonderful party that went on long into the night. Finally, looking out the window, we noticed a tranquil snowfall brewing.

Jun-il's room would continue to be a spiritual haven that greeted me warmly.

One evening, I finally told him what had been on my mind for so long. "Jun-il," I said, "I have a dilemma. Our family wants to emigrate from Korea, to escape all of the problems that have plagued us here. We applied for one program, but it did not work out. My father is drowning in frustration to leave this country, and I now feel suffocated in our current position. What do you think of this plan? Do you think we have gone mad?" I asked him anxiously.

"I think it's a great idea. If I had the chance, I would leave, too. It is a brilliant idea. Your father is a man of foresight. If I were you, I would continue to look for a way to leave the country. In a way, leaving Korea is the most patriotic thing you can do! Frankly speaking, I would like to fly away from this wretched place. Damn the history! Damn the poverty!" His words encouraged me to keep pursuing the plan.

As time elapsed, I became increasingly frustrated with our lack of progress. The idea of emigrating kept me from moving forward in my present life. It was as if I were suspended in a black hole. I got more and more impatient. At length, I realized that I could no longer wait for an opportunity to present itself. I needed to do something about the situation.

One morning, in the spring of 1962, I happened to be leafing through a newspaper. An article about a civil rights leader caught my eye. Ham Seuk Heon was to speak at a high school in a suburban area outside of Seoul. For no particular reason, I felt drawn to go to hear him speak. When I arrived, the assembly hall of the school was crowded with people. I was attracted by the applauding audience. Ham Seuk Heon was a very charismatic man in his late sixties, with long, white hair and a wavy, silver beard. He spoke of the righteous life of the great man, Mr. Lee Sang Jae, who had been the spiritual mainstay of the Korean people during the Japanese plundering of the Korean peninsula. Ham Seuk Heon's fiery eloquence connected with the spirit of the crowd, which resulted in thunderous applause.

"Ladies and gentlemen!" he began. "The present military occupation of our nation is tantamount to robbery. An ancient sage, Lao-tzu, said: 'The world cannot be ruled by only one military force.' Look at world history. Every nation that has brandished a sword has shared the same fate. There have been no exceptions. Alexander the Great, the great Roman Empire, the great Japanese imperialism. The list goes on and on. Military powers love to use the word 'great,' and it has been their ruin."

In addition to his historical observations, Ham Seuk Heon particularly emphasized that Christianity should be magnanimous to other religions. He continued to impress the crowd. However, as he began to comment on Korean history, his voice raised in anger: "Korea has the history of a Gal-Bo ("*harlot*")! She has been a poor prostitute who has been repeatedly raped by brutal outsiders. Now this country has broken again into two. The little Korean peninsula has been crucified for too long. How long will the poor Gal-Bo be forced to hang on the cross? We have to wake up from our slumber. Only a living soul can save us from this disgraceful history." He spoke in shocking terms without pause. At times, he quoted the doctrine of ahimsa of the great mentor of India, Karamchand Ghandi. Though his language appeared to be cynical, Ham Seuk Heon defiantly struck a chord with the masses, who had led hard lives in uncertain times since the division of Korea. His words were as refreshing to the ears of the crowd as were John the Baptist's words many years ago. He seemed to be a supreme being with a transcendental attitude about death. His messages clarified a new gospel that was different from the trite dogmas of the established religions.

After hearing Ham Seuk Heon for the first time, I never missed another one of his speeches. At the threshold of my adulthood, he showed me another way of looking at life. I thought that he might be the great mentor for Korea during those divided times. Most importantly, he was able to rouse me out of my trance by giving me hope that I could be liberated from my intangible pressures. I had been spending my early adulthood drifting in an empty dream, longing for a mental escape.

In the summer of 1966 when I graduated from the college, I was drafted into the army.

An Ugly World

On a rainy afternoon in August of 1966, I found myself among a multitude of army recruit candidates being jostled on a southbound army train. I shared a seat with two other draftees; one was a middle school teacher, the other an artist. Due to the grave atmosphere, we instantly became close to one another. "We need to help each other. Wherever we go, whatever happens in the future, we all have the same destiny." The three of us swore an oath to each other. It was a jet-black night, and we did not know our destination.

The moment I stepped into the dark army camp, I felt my flesh crawl and my soul leave the human world, as though I had descended into hell. After two weeks of being held like a miserable prisoner, I was moved from that temporary camp. The new training camp was to be my house of discipline for the next six weeks. It was raining in buckets onto the bare ground leading to the new barrack. The torrential rain changed the dry, hard soil into a sticky, wet dough. My feet were continually ankle-deep in the well-kneaded mud. Reduced to a wet, miserable rat, I was dragged to boot camp.

"Attention!" came a voice. "I am your staff sergeant. Listen to me. From now on, you are no longer human beings! You are objects! For six weeks you will go through rigorous training! You will not fail! You will follow my orders or you will be punished! Do you understand?" The fresh young draftees stood stiff with fear. My heart sank at his speech. After a pause, he issued an initial order to his inferiors, "Strip down to your underwear. Put all of your personal belongings in here," pointing to a large bucket. "If you hide anything, you will not be forgiven." The boss stood by looking intimidating. I gave up everything except a little emergency money that I had hidden in my underwear. Despite the risk of discovery, I was unwilling to give up the secret fund that Mother had given me. The staff sergeant grinned treacherously at my awkward gestures, but did not check inside my underpants. I sighed inwardly. The man meticulously examined each recruits' belongings.

Having removed our civilian clothes, we were ordered to put on the used green army uniforms that were staked up in the corner of the room. "Hurry up! You have five minutes, and then stand up on the floor!" The sergeant scrupulously began to examine each face as we stood at attention. "You! Come out of line. You may stay next to me. You will be a liaison recruit. You are a lucky man." He appointed me to be his personal secretary. He continued to examine the faces of the recruits, who were frozen with fear. "You! Step forward! From now on, you are the leader of your fellow men! Understand?" Surprisingly, he had picked Hyeung-Tae, with whom I had been sitting next to on the train! I had to smile that my buddy had been picked as a leader. The staff sergeant nominated four more squad leaders. As he completed the organization of his platoon, he gave us strict instructions. "Listen! You will obey your new leaders and follow their instructions. As I said already, you are not humans anymore. You are all just cogs in a machine. Remember you are now property of the nation. Your past is to be forgotten!" He spoke to us as though he was our master and we were dogs.

One evening, all of the exhausted trainees slid onto their wadded mattress, ready for sweet sleep. All lights were out, except for one dim bulb that clung to the ceiling of the quarters. Just as sleep was about to take over, the staff sergeant burst into the room, yelling, "Get up, you scum! Get up! All leaders out here! Put your faces on the ground! Two canteens are lost! I don't know who stole them. Do you? Those canteens were made in the USA. How much do you think they cost in US currency? You are all liable for the loss. You leaders are responsible for your men, so you will be punished!" He then pointed to me and shouted, "Hey you! Fetch me a long thick branch from outside."

The sergeant began to ruthlessly thrash their buttocks. The chief leader of the platoon, my friend Hyeung-Tae, and the four squad leaders, writhed on the bare ground in pain. They curled their bodies into rolls, like caterpillars, while their colleagues looked on in horror. "Get up!" the sergeant shouted. "If you want to sleep tonight, you must fix this problem quickly! I will come back in one hour, so this had better be resolved!" As he left the barracks, his agents, including Hyeung-Tae, turned on their fellow men. They came on as if they were mad dogs and used even more abusive words than the sergeant had used. Consequently, most of the trainees were forced to give up their emergency funds. Those who could not come up with any money were selected to be offered to the boss for a beating. An hour later, when the staff sergeant returned to his newly-appointed leaders, he was presented with the money that had been extorted in his absence. The sergeant tried to accept the money with reluctance but was unable to suppress the grin from his lips, knowing that he was being given free cash.

"Thank you for your quick cooperation in this unfortunate event. I hope that this kind of thing will never happen again. After all, we are all war buddies, and we all need to help each other. Good job, everybody. Now get to sleep." He spoke to his loyal followers with honey-coated words, and played the part of the magnanimous leader.

After all of the trainees had fallen asleep, he woke me out of my own dead slumber, saying, "Hey you, wake up! Tell the leaders to come here." He had already prepared a little party of rice wine and chunks of boiled pork. "Sit, please relax. Let's have a drink together. I am glad to find that you have already adopted the military spirit." Looking like the cat that ate the canary, our shrewd master urged his chosen disciples to have a drink. "Toast! Toast! For our eternal comradeship!" He lifted his cup high, careful to speak in a voice that would not wake the trainees, who were all sleeping as if death had overtaken them.

That was not to be the last of such "events." They seemed to happen at regular intervals. It appeared to me that the staff sergeant enjoyed watching the men turn on one another. With each "problem," his loyal agents acted with deft precision and reveled in their supreme authority. I was lucky enough to be protected by my favorable position as the first sergeant's personal liaison recruit. Hyeung-Tae, a man with whom I shared a blood oath, began to glare at me hatefully. He had become very good at his job; it was as if he had been transformed into a very shrewd dog who could mercilessly tear off the raw flesh of his colleagues.

As all of this took place, the emergency funds that the recruits had brought from home were drained. The first sergeant began to get frustrated and started using the trainees' chests as target practice for his martial arts. Wearing his heavy army boots, he would jump in the air and kick the men in the chest. "Bastard! This guy is crazy! This is not army training; this is torture!" I shook in anger, but our six-week training was coming to a close. Late one evening, a senior sergeant of the company came into our quarters carrying a large yellow envelope.

"Listen, everyone, sit quietly on the floor," he said. "As I call your name, come up one by one." We were each paid a meager monthly wage. I was deeply inspired by this unexpected income. It was the first positive thing that had happened since being reborn in this strange new world. Every trainee hid his precious money in his own secret place, then laid his dead-tired body down to sleep.

Shortly after the senior sergeant left our barracks, I was awakened from a sound sleep by someone's screaming. I jumped up as heavy shoes were kicking my head. "All of you! Get up!" The staff sergeant had found fault with the recruits again. "Listen to me!" he bellowed. "Our army blankets were stolen again! I don't know when. Even if I collected all of your wages that were paid this evening, I don't think you could compensate for this loss." I instantly knew that we were going to have to give up our wages. The atmosphere immediately became tense again. The subordinate leaders extorted their fellow trainees out of their first army income. In less than half an hour, our meager wages had gone to hell. Even though I was deadly weary, I could not sleep for an unknown bitterness.

As the training course drew to an end, our leader's arrogant attitude changed. He seemed to be trying to appease his subordinates. He would occasionally make jokes bordering on flattery. As if he hoped we would forget the robbery and torture he had inflicted for the past forty-five days. He must have been worried that we might complain after we were released from his leadership. Finally, a ceremony was held at regimental headquarters to mark the completion of our training. I was so dizzy with the sense of liberation that I felt as though I were flying away from the gates of hell. At that same moment, I stole a glance at the staff sergeant who had come with us as a guide. I was surprised to see that he had tears flowing down his cheeks. What was the meaning of this? Did he regret that he had not stolen more money from us while we were held hostage under his command? Or was it possibly an expression of humanity? Was he remorseful of the atrocities he had committed? To this day, I have not solved the mystery of his perplexing tears.

In the last days of October 1966, when the dead leaves were dancing wildly in the late autumn breeze, I took a train to my new army post. The first night I spent there was not agreeable. I arrived too late for dinner and could hardly sleep from hunger. I stole out of bed and snuck into the army kitchen like a sharp-set night mouse. I knocked on the door with caution. There was no reply. Hunger drove me to repeatedly pound my fist on the door. "Who the hell is it?" a gruff voice said from beyond. "Do you have any idea how late it is? Get the hell out of here!"

I replied, "Sir, I am a new soldier to this unit. I am starving. Can you please spare a scrap of food?" I was pleading as though I were a helpless old beggar.

"Wait there, you asshole!" came the sour reply. A shadowy figure appeared in the doorway, and a roll wrapped in old newspaper was thrust toward me "Here, take this. Now get lost. If you come and bother me again, I'll break your head!"

I snatched the crumpled bundle with the swiftness of a raven stealing from a rat. While I walked under the starry sky on my way back to my quarters, I opened the bundle and noticed that he had filled it with the scorched rice. Then, I proceeded to split the rice bundles in two, and I stuffed each lump into a pocket. After climbing back into bed, I bit into the hardened block of rice. Ignoring the bitter taste, I chewed the hard rice until dawn.

After a few days of waiting around the barracks of the army division, I was finally given an assignment. I was to report to a unit perched on the highest hill of the division. My duty was to fetch the meals for all the soldiers senior to me. I had to get these meals three times a day from the army kitchen, which was at the foot of a hill far away from my own unit. My own portions were always scanty; therefore, I would quickly dash for any leftovers, like a scavenger, when senior soldiers finished their meals.

One cloudless morning, I was able to volunteer in a program that helped farmers who were short of laborers for their harvest. A sea of golden rice straws undulated in the breeze. I was overwhelmed with a crowning sense of liberation, as though I had been released from prison. I was led to a thatched village where fruit trees, heavy with scarlet persimmons, were scattered about. Nakdong River glinted in the distance. I was put to work helping with the threshing machine. The farmer provided a lunch of newly-threshed rice and freshly-picked vegetables. I voraciously shoveled a bowl of boiled rice into my mouth without pausing to chew; well, that is until rice grains started popping out of my choked throat. For the first time in many, many days, I had a feeling of satiety, which led to a sense of euphoria.

A few days before the New Year, I got a surprise visit from

my father. He silently sat and listened to my tales of woe. The only visible sign of emotion was his staring at me with tears in his eyes. That evening, I said goodbye to him at the local railroad station. In the vacant square adjacent to the station, a little gingko tree was shivering in the setting sun.

A Chosen Man

On an icy morning in January of 1967, I was called into the office of the signal captain. "Private Kim," he said, "our unit has been ordered to pick one corpsman for dispatching to the Vietnam War. I think you are the right person for the job. It would be very honorable for our unit if you would accept this offer. I understand that there is wonderful food in Vietnam, and that a combat stipend is issued. This may be a good opportunity for you, so please, think about my proposal and give me your answer in the morning." Captain Lee had a very resolute look on his face and a persuasive manner. I spent a sleepless night contemplating his tempting idea. More than anything, I wanted to escape the hunger and stress of my present circumstances. As day broke, I scurried into the captain's office. Springing to his feet, he asked, "Did you make up your mind, Private Kim?"

"Yes, sir. I will go," I answered simply.

"Thank you, Private Kim, for volunteering. I will report this to my superiors. Just relax until you receive your next orders." He seemed to emphasize that I had "volunteered." Truth be told, it was half volunteering and half compulsion.

A few days later, I was shipped off. Twenty-four soldiers

who had been chosen from different units of the same division were lined up in front of the divisional headquarters. A portly little commander with two silver stars on his shoulders emerged in a dignified manner. "Attention! Salute the Commander!" ordered a lieutenant colonel, breaking the serenity of the cold, crisp dawn.

"Stand at ease," the commander said in a solemn tone. "Fellow soldiers! I wish you glorious military merits and good health until you return home!" Then the general began shaking hands with each soldier. Suddenly, in the middle of the ceremony, a soldier in his thirties burst out sobbing. The general stopped in front of the crying man. "What's wrong, soldier?" asked the commander, eyeing him suspiciously.

"Sir, Commander! I am a married man with two children and a widowed old mother. If I die, they are going to starve to death. I am not a volunteer. My senior officer ordered me to come here. Please, Commander! Stop me from being sent to Vietnam." The soldier appealed to the General in a trembling voice. For a moment, silence fell heavily upon us all.

Finally, the General broke the spell. He spoke to the soldier in a soothing, hushed voice. "Soldier, you are a chosen man. You will be paid for your special mission. You will be able to drink as much good beer as you want. Do you understand what I'm saying?" As soon as the commander finished his admonition, one of his staff officers hurried to finish the farewell ceremony in an effort to avoid another awkward incident. "Attention! Salute the commander!" Concurrently with a scream of the senior officer, an icy order fell on the chosen soldiers. "Get in the truck! Hurry up!" I immediately jumped into a truck that was standing by like a funeral limousine, ready to transport us to our next incarnation. The freezing wind pushed through the torn holes of the tarpaulin covering the truck. The steam from my mouth created a white mist. My teeth rattled striking the upper part against the lower part.

"Damn this cold weather!" one of the soldiers complained. "It must be more than twenty degrees below zero! Where the hell are we going now?" At dusk we were dumped at an unknown army camp. My frozen body thawed and I soon fell into a sound sleep. During my short spell of slumber I had a strange dream. A little blue bird, locked in a steel cage, was trying to escape from its barred cell. That same night, I was forced to take yet another army train to yet another unknown destination. Some servicemen were making a hushed stir under a dim light hanging from the ceiling. I sat next to a corporal, who sat silently without meeting my gaze. Prompted by curiosity, I had an itch to talk to him.

"Do you have any special reason to go to Vietnam?" I enquired, looking cautiously into his face.

After a short pause, he reluctantly spoke, turning his head toward the window. "No reason in particular," he said. "I have only six months before I complete my service. I don't know exactly why I volunteered. To be frank, I have no place to go after I am discharged. I'm an orphan. I lost both my parents during the Korean War." After he finished muttering to himself, he went silent again.

As dawn arrived, I got off the train at a local station in the capital city of Seoul. It was bitterly cold. I mixed with other soldiers, who were jumping up and down to keep their bodies from freezing. In a corner of the railroad station, a covered carriage was serving hot noodle soup and some simple side dishes. Business there was flourishing. I was able to wedge myself between the throngs of people into a narrow space in the cart. As I stepped into the wagon, I was engulfed in the hot steam rising from the pot. The sweet smell of warm noodle soup intensified my hunger pains. Although I had no money, I held my ground in that crowded spot, continuously edging forward. I looked nervously around, hoping to find someone who could loan me some spare change so I could buy a bowl. As I was getting closer, my hope of finding that savior was fading. Then, out of nowhere, I heard the most pleasant voice. “Private Kim! Come here. Why don’t you have a bowl of hot noodle soup? Don’t worry; it’s on me.” It was Corporal Lee, whom I had sat next to on the train. Without waiting for my response, he ordered me a bowl of soup. His act of generosity and fraternity brought tears to my eyes. That bowl of hot noodle soup not only saved my pinched guts, but also brought back my faith in humanity.

I soon acclimated to our new, dismal encampment that, like a POW camp, was surrounded by barbed wire. Each man had his own method of dealing with his stay in the temporary camp. Some would slaughter the lice they ferreted out of their underwear. They would squish the offending bugs, one by one, between the fingernails of their two thumbs. One man resembled an autistic patient, sitting in a corner in his own silent world. Others would pick fights with each other. I, on the other hand, became a chain-smoker. I would desperately smoke the butt of a cigarette to its end, until the burning tobacco scorched my lips. The smoke from the tobacco made me sink into a sea of oblivion, momentarily letting me escape from my past regrets. While I drew the smoke deep into my lungs, I’d fall into a sweet moment of fuzzy consciousness. The sensation would start at the top of my head and would radiate all the way to my toes. When I ran out of cigarettes, I was quickly transformed into a mongrel. I dug in trash cans and rummaged in every corner of the camp, looking for discarded cigarette butts.

As dusk gathered one evening, I found myself on another army train, traveling at night. I arrived at the local station, Chun-Cheun, early in the morning. The very moment the train was brought to a standstill, a local woman peddler arrived. She was a middle-aged woman with a large earthenware steamer that she carried on top of her head as she came running close to the train. The lady had hot, steamed rice cakes topped with squashed red beans. She was quickly surrounded by a swarm of soldiers. In exchange for her hot cooked rice cakes, soldiers gave her raw rice grains that they had received from their previous units. Though I had no rice with which to barter, I forced my way to the front of the crowd. I stuffed one whole hot rice cake into my mouth, grabbed another, and ran as fast as I could. "Money! Money! Give me my money!" her protest trailed after me, as if she were heaping a curse on my head. I quickly regretted what I had done to the poor lady. "Someday," I resolved, "I will repay this debt threefold."

After some time, our army truck, filled with soldiers, slowed to a crawl. We rattled up and down narrow, twisting, rugged mountain paths that were buried in a sea of greenish bushes. Every time the truck went around a sharp curve, we would dangle over the edge of some precipitous cliff, causing me to draw a sharp breath, hoping for the best. A soldier sitting next to me thought this would be a good time to nudge me in my ribs and complain about our situation: "Where on earth are they taking us now? Do you know? I am guessing we are going to a guerrilla-training center. And for what? The government says that we are going to fight for freedom and peace. Do you believe that shit? They are selling our blood for money. We are hired soldiers. We are no longer human. We are nothing but cows being led to slaughter. Private Kim, do you get what I'm talking about?"

It occurred to me that he was a very cynical person. "I don't know anything," I said in a sarcastic tone, to cut his diatribe short, "because I am just a cow that belongs to the army." He gave me a bitter smile and stopped talking.

The mountains seemed endless. Every white-capped mountaintop towered toward heaven, as if vying for attention. The fleeting glimpses of the remote mountain peaks put me in a pensive mood. "Am I really going to war? To sell my life? For whom?" I muttered to myself.

Late at night, we reached our destination. We had been brought to a deep valley. My transition camp was built on a relatively flat floor close to a mountain creek. The creek had a hard-frozen crust, under which the stream could be heard trickling down. The fresh air and repetitive sound of the water was a soothing backdrop to the wild, natural setting of the encampment. Over the next several weeks of our fanatic training course, the valleys became stalled by snow. Before our long journey to Vietnam, every soldier was provided with a new uniform. It was as if we had already died and were given our funeral shrouds to wear to our next incarnation. As a token of our transition, we each received our war wages and were granted a special overnight leave from the camp.

As luck would have it, I got sick that night. While everybody else was living it up in the mountain villages, I was crouched in pain next to a lukewarm coal stove. The next morning, a short ceremony, marking our passage from encampment to war, was held on the open drill field. Soon, an array of army trucks began to parade toward us. After we were all loaded into the long line of vehicles, we made our way out of the valley, plowing through the snow-covered road, around the mountain and out of the winding mountain pass. We finally reached the railroad station at Chun-Cheun. A long black serpent of a train awaited us. We were soon swallowed whole into the extended, empty belly of the metal beast.

The platform was jammed to capacity with people rushing to the windows of the train, trying to catch a glimpse of loved ones. In the clamoring chaos, an army band bellowed vehemently while a group of female students fervently sang "Song of Victory" as they waved small Korean flags. From my seat on the train, I could simultaneously see a sobbing, grizzled-haired couple in their seventies, a woman with a baby strapped to her back, searching for her husband, and a young woman brimming over with tears, seeing off her young lover. The metallic snake started to come alive with the sounds of whistles, announcing its wish to begin the long journey southward. The melded voices and pain-stricken cries of those left behind, rang in my head for a long time. I closed my eyes and slipped into a somber mood.

I dozed off into a dreamy world for a while. The train drew up to the platform of the Chung-Ryang-Ri station on the outskirts of Seoul. Snowflakes and pellets of sleet seemed to be attacking me, but I was protected by my window. People had already flooded the platform. An army band was playing as the conductor swung his baton spasmodically under the dismal sky. In spite of myself, I was compelled to see what was going on. I lifted the window sash and, at the very moment my head started to venture out, somebody's fist met my face.

"Son of a bitch!" a young first lieutenant yelled at me. "Who told you to open the window?" A lavish amount of blood was streaming down my chin. I was instantly ashamed of myself.

"Hey! God damn you!" shouted out my uncle from several yards away. He was among the crowd and was not happy with the young officer who had hit me in the face. Soon, all the windows were open. People rushed to the windows to see their loved ones. One of my brothers was able to pass me hot sweet potatoes that had been wrapped in old newspapers, but, thanks to the unexpected attack from the young officer, my right upper tooth was loose, and I wasn't able to eat them. On seeing my family, particularly my mother, I couldn't help feeling a sense of shame. At that moment, an old Red Cross lady approached me, extending a cup of hot black tea. "Hello soldier," she said, "why don't you have a cup of tea? Oh my, you are bleeding from the mouth. Are you okay?" She did her best to thaw my frozen heart. The warm tea helped to relieve my anger.

Soon, the train rolled away again. We were headed for a harbor city at the edge of the southern land. It would be our last stop. As I sat facing the open sea, sipping my hot tea, I began thinking about my uncle who had gone to the front line just before the Korean War. "I may be falling prey to a new epoch," I muttered to myself like a fatalist. "I could become a victim just as my uncle did." The train kept clattering at full speed.

As we pulled into the port city of Pusan, there was a rift in the claret-colored clouds and the pale dawn glimmered ominously. In the distance, the water shone eerily with a greenish-blue tint. At dockside, a gigantic US naval transport ship was floating with its expandable jaw opened like a shark waiting to swallow the whole bodies of men. After the mammoth creature had finished gulping a number of young, smaller creatures, the hulking body sluggishly took off for the open sea. Against the background noise of the ship's horns, a flock of seagulls circled our bow. It was as if they were bidding me a farewell.

As we reached the open sea, the giant ship began to pitch and roll, causing me to become seasick. I spent the entire trip to Vietnam pacing the deck from prow to stern. I would sometimes watch absentmindedly as dolphins jumped like acrobats against the distant horizon, or as flying fishes skimmed over the water, racing our giant vessel. After a few days of tedious travel, the colossal ship anchored its heavy body. Dark blue mountaintops towered in the distance. Somebody exclaimed, "Look! They are exactly the same as mountains in Korea!" I was suddenly overcome with a fit of anxiety. I instinctively fingered the black rosary hanging around my neck. I held the metal cross of the rosary and simply prayed, feeling like a drowning man clutching at straws.

An army band played enthusiastically as we made our way ashore. The sunlight was glaring down upon us as if trying to incinerate all of the earthly creatures it touched. A sergeant screamed, "All aboard!" and our trucks moved out, creating a misty cloud of dust as we moved toward the Vienhoa airport. Once we reached the airbase, an American army airplane immediately snatched us up. As if it were a celestial bird, it flew southward toward the burning sun. "To the valley of death?" I wondered. "No choice but to resign myself to destiny." Many thoughts crowded my mind as we touched down at the Tanson Nhat airport in Saigon City. Many soldiers from the U.S. and other countries were bustling about. Some of them dozed, leaning on their bags, with the distant boom of guns as their languid lullaby.

I was assigned to a division stationed on the outskirts of Saigon City. After a few days, I volunteered for a frontline mission. We dug into the sandy soil, building a half-underground camp, using sandbags and soil as our walls. The defensive position in which I was buried was located near the small village of Vihntuan. During the day, soldiers of the construction engineer corps went out of their position to work on road improvements. Some of the soldiers would go to the village of Vihntuan and provide the villagers with flour or cooking oil made in the USA. This worked as public welfare as well as a pacification effort.

I shared a trench with a first sergeant named Mr. Choi. He was in his late thirties and was skinny and had prominent cheekbones. When we had downtime, he liked to make idle conversation. "Private Kim," he asked one day, "why did you come to Vietnam? Did you volunteer, or was it a compulsory mandate from above?" He has a crooked smile on this face.

"Half and half, sir. How about you?" I said.

"Me? I volunteered. I am but a poor soldier. I recently married and have one child. I need the extra war benefit. Even during the most moments of the Korean War, I survived. I think I am a lucky man. At the end of 1952, my battalion was almost totally wiped out. Only a few of us survived. Did you know that the smell of rotten corpses brings on a splitting headache? The smell is like that of soybean sauce. Most of my Korean War buddies were young, like you. But the Vietnam War seems to be different. There is no distinction between the front line and the rear. At any time, you and I could be overtaken by Vietcong.

"As you know, during the day, Vihntuan village is under the control of the Republic of South Vietnam, but as night falls, the village turns into the Vietcong. Private Kim, are you ready to die now?"

First sergeant Choi had reeled off his personal war

philosophy. I said bluntly, "I am not ready to die, sir. I have a lot to look forward to in the future."

"Tonight, or tomorrow night, we may meet our fates. Then you and I will be eternally linked as we go toward the Kingdom of Heaven!" Mr. Choi laughed as he teased me.

During the daytime, everything looked peaceful. However, as the shadows of night came near, the whizzing sound of bullets could be heard, not to stop until dawn rose again. As the days rolled by, the gunshots sounded like the buzzing of idle hornets. I began to grow accustomed to the callousness of war. Thirteen months passed and before I knew it; my Vietnam duty was drawing to an end.

A Soldier's Death

A few days before the lunar New Year, in February of 1968, I was to leave Vietnam. Before I left the front line, my buddy, Corporal Lee, took over my signal duty. I was soon withdrawn from trench life in order to be repositioned with the main force so that arrangements could be made for my return home. Early on a dull morning, the day before the lunar New Year, a procession of army trucks carried us through the heavily-misted village of Dian. As we passed down the dusty road, ashy gravestones could be seen bobbing up and down in the murky fog, like apparitions, haunting me with a mysterious chill. It was as if they were rushing at me, cursing, "Why did you come to our country? To kill us? For money? Was it a joke? What was the point?" The soundless howls seemed to carry through the thick mist, piercing my imagination.

That day, I was flown to the Nahtrang district to board an American transport ship for home. While we were being hidden deep in an unknown mountain, bad news reached us. The so-called Lunar New Year's offensive had taken place. It was an all-out attack from North Vietnam. The Vietcong who had been submerged in South Vietnam attacked at the same time. What shocked me the most was the news that the area where I had been positioned for thirteen months had been blasted by the local Vietcong. My dear friend, Corporal Lee, who had been assigned to my signal job, had been blown to pieces. I ached at the news of his death. Guilt ate at my conscience. He had died in my place.

Corporal Lee had been a fun, happy fellow who always made people feel good. Once in a while, we would have beer parties in his dugout. Sometimes, after we'd had a couple of beers, he would tell me stories from his personal life. He would even talk about his private love story. He said that he had lost both his parents in his early childhood. Before his conscription, he had lived with his only sibling. He became depressed when talking about his unhappy past, but when it came to chatting about his lover, he became happy as a clam. "Corporal Lee," I would say, "tell me about your lover. Is she pretty?"

"Hey! Don't talk like that," he would answer. "We are still in platonic love. We have not even consummated our relationship! I met her at university; she is my first love. She promised to marry me after I am discharged. Kim, we need to keep in touch after we are discharged from the army. I want you to come to our wedding. You have to remember, after all, we are war buddies." He would beam at me, pushing out his white, side tooth.

"Of course I'll come to your wedding!" I echoed his innocent sentiment with delight. On that fateful lunar New Year's Day, we parted ways forever. With his death and shattered dreams buried in my heart, I was on my way home.

When I arrived back on the shore of my homeland, I imagined that a flock of seagulls were greeting both me and Corporal Lee. The birds whirled above the quarterdeck with their wings quivering in the wind. A sense of delight, mixed with a misty sorrow, enveloped me.

I was granted a special furlough for three weeks and was filled with a sense of relieved happiness, like a bird that had been released from its cage. From time to time, the face of Corporal Lee would drift in and out of my vision. On yet another early, bitter morning, I got off a train at the Seoul Railroad station. I hurried to board a street bus bound for my home. Instantly, I felt a sense of tension in the air. In a frenzied voice, a radio announcer screamed that a state of national emergency was in effect. He shouted: "A band of North Korean guerrillas has attacked the President's residence. Some of the guerrillas escaped, our forces killed some, and one of them, Shin Cho Kim, surrendered voluntarily. The army is continuing to search for the other guerrillas. Due to these events, the present term for those in the armed services will be extended for another six months."

The breaking news stunned me. "Shit! On this day of all days, I return home to another Korean War!" Adding insult to injury, this meant that my discharge would be delayed. An ominous premonition weighed on me. When my father finally saw me, he greeted me with a smile. He must have worried that I would not return. However, then he started to speak to me, his face changed from a smile to a serious look. "You know," he said, "Korea and Vietnam are in the same war."

One day, at my father's request, I made a courtesy visit to one of my relatives who belonged to the wealthiest class, and who had a powerful connection with the military government. As I bowed politely to him, he threw me an odd question. He grinned and asked, "Did you make a lot of money in Vietnam?" My meager monthly war stipend of $37.50 flashed before my eyes. I was so shocked by his question that I became dumbstruck. "Of all the questions to ask me, he talks about money," I thought. I shuddered at his insult. This disturbing visit, as well as hearing about the military service extension, aggravated my furlough.

One day, with a deep regret, I visited the national cemetery where my friend, Corporal Lee, was buried. In bitter grief, I stared at the vision of him for a very long time.

A Nun Named Mary

After my return from Vietnam, I found that I tired very easily. It was not long before I was posted to my new military unit. The company chose me for the ranger-training course. The rugged alpine drill was beyond my capability. The result of the hard physical training was an unspecified illness. An army doctor recommended that I be admitted to a large army hospital. There, I was issued a loose, blue, patient's clothing, which looked like a prison uniform. I was assigned to a cozy corner bed next to a window. I could see the blue sky and, occasionally, observe some naive flying bugs that would crash against the window, producing a cracking noise before falling down.

In the bed next to mine was a soldier lying in a state of unconsciousness. His face had turned dark brown and his body was reduced to skin and bones. He was put on the danger list, reserved for patients who were terminally ill. The name tag at the end of his bed read: "Private, Kim Byung-Song." Sometimes an aide would stop by Private Kim's bed and scowl at him. On a metal shelf beside his bed was a small, crumpled, green bag. I was equally concerned and curious about my neighbor. "Where is he from? How did he get sick?" I wondered. I went to him and felt his boney finger and wondered if he could survive or not. I watched him as he struggled in absolute isolation; I recalled the sad karma that had befallen my friend, Corporal Lee.

One morning, a few days after I had been admitted to the hospital, Private Kim's skinny body squirmed, and he tried to open his eyes. I immediately went to his side and looked at him. He wore a faint smile on his pale complexion. His lips were dry and crooked, as if he were trying to speak. Though he couldn't manage to utter a word, I could easily read his lips. His final words were: "Good-bye. So long." He then closed his eyes for the last time and lapsed into eternal serenity. His death was quickly reported to those in charge. Neither the doctor nor the nurse in charge of the ward came when Private Kim died. The only people who came were two soldiers who put a new, green uniform on the dead Private Kim. They tied his hands and feet tightly with rope. They stuffed his ears and nostrils with cotton and, lastly, wrapped his head with a white cloth. They moved his corpse to the morgue, where he would soon be turned to ash.

After they had taken Private Kim away, I noticed that his small, old bag remained. I opened the bag with care. It contained a crumpled letter, a small black Bible, an old toothbrush, and a worn washcloth. These were the only traces that Private Kim had ever existed. The letter had been written by his younger sister. It read:

Dear Brother,

I was delighted to receive your letter. I am glad that you are finished with your training. Father and Mother are deeply upset to hear that you are sick. What happened to your health? You were always healthy when you were home. Are you seriously ill?

As you demanded, our parents asked everybody on the island to borrow from them money; however, they were unable to get anything. I do not blame our neighbors as they are all poor as well. Father and Mother have become very depressed. Dear Brother, forgive us, but I'm wondering why you have to buy your own medicine. I know you say that some of your fellow patients have to buy medicine from the civilian pharmacy with money sent from their parents, but shouldn't the army provide free care for their own soldiers? I am so sorry, Brother! The only thing I can do now is to pray to God. Our parents are constantly in tears. My dear Brother! Please do not be discouraged, and try to overcome your present hardships! Brother, I long for the day you return home in good health.

Love, your little sister,
Sunok

After reading that letter, I choked to hold back my tears. His vacant bed was quickly occupied by another patient, who had been a member of the military police unit close to the 38th parallel.

Dull days passed by. Then, one bright afternoon, a young nun wearing a black veil visited me. "How are you, brother?" the Catholic nun asked in a clear, bright voice.

"I'm okay," I responded awkwardly.

"Is there anything I can do to help you?" she asked.

"Nothing," I responded, bluntly.

"Do you believe in God?"

"I don't know," I answered coldly.

"What do you mean, 'I don't know?'"

"Because I don't really care about such things," I retorted.

"Why not?"

"You know," I responded, "history tells us that religion keeps the innocent quiet by promising them compensation in the next world. I think this life is more important than the next."

"You may be right, brother. Either way, we are under God's control. You know that, because God created us. Only through our Lord in Heaven can we be saved," she added.

"I am not against Christianity. In fact, I am pro-Christian. I trust in Jesus regardless of whether he was resurrected or not. But, I have a different viewpoint regarding the Christian dogmas. I understand that the truth cannot be monopolized by any one religious sect, and that everybody can hold the key to the Kingdom of Heaven. Let's use the tragic example of the division of the Korean peninsula. The division of Korea was caused, in large part, by the alienation of people due to an ideological concept. That self-righteousness is likely to breed exclusionism. Eventually, exclusionism brings a bloody conflict. I believe in only a common Lord, and not an exclusive God."

The nun responded, "Brother! You think too much! You look tired, and you need rest." She had not looked at me antagonistically through my long, rude refutation. I felt rather ashamed of myself as she scrutinized my face. Her tranquil smile made my stiff mind ease a bit.

After that, she visited me regularly. She came once a week, usually on Wednesday afternoons. One day, Mary brought me a book entitled, *"The Paramita of the East and the West."* The book was about many ancient philosophers and religious originators. One Korean Buddhist priest in particular, Seu-San (*"western mountain"*), impressed me. Seu-San had lived in the 17th century.

"What do you think of the book I loaned you?" she asked.

"Quite an impressive book," I replied in a friendly voice. Somehow I felt at ease every time I looked at her face.

I began to long for her visits. Her sparkling, dark eyes and her soft voice were imprinted in my mind. "Brother," she said one day, "why don't you come to the Catholic Church in the hospital? I am sure our Lord will respond to your prayers." I nodded my head at her as a token of acceptance of her proposal. My instant response obviously filled her with delight. "Thank you, brother! I wish our Lord of Heaven will bless you."

As she had requested, I attended the next Sunday morning service. Frankly speaking, I wanted to be closer to her, rather than to God. "Brother," she said afterwards, "take care of yourself. I will see you next week." As always, Mary made a point of giving me a tender word of consolation when we parted. But, without any warning, I was suddenly transferred to a remote army hospital. I missed the woman who had cleared my cloudy spirit with her bright crystal soul. The night I was admitted to that hospital, I dreamed of the mysterious woman, Mary Magdelene, who looked into my empty tomb. "Don't go away," I called in a muffled voice, "I have something to tell you."

"Hello, brother! I wish I could cast off my veiled garment. I want to return as an ordinary woman who can be touched by real human flesh. Goodbye, goodbye..." As soon as the strange lady stopped speaking, she turned into a huge bird shrouded in a white veil, and flew into the distant sky. I was left to watch her ascension to Heaven. Though my acquaintance with the nun, Mary, had been short, it left an indelible mark on me.

Becoming Human Again

My military service was finally coming to an end. I could see the light at the far end of a long, black tunnel. It had been a journey of 1,085 days. It was a bright, sunny morning, and I was full of optimism. It was a day I had thought would never come. My worry was that this day was only a dream. Even after my discharge, I was haunted by nightmares. I would writhe in desperate agony, trying to escape the barracks again.

"I have completed my three-year obligation! Why are you drafting me again?" I would scream at the top of my voice, in my dreams, railing against my recall. When I awoke from the dreams I would heave a long sigh of relief. In the long run, I did become human again.

The reality of the political landscape never let me fully enjoy the freedom of my release from the army. Father was just as anxious as before.

"This country is hopeless; military hooligans have already begun to squeeze the life out of people. We should escape from here." Day in and day out, father continued to pressure me about fleeing the country. I wandered the streets with empty pockets, searching for a way to escape my hardship. Whenever

I would get really depressed, I would visit a Catholic Church to remind me of my dear nun, Mary, who used to console me with her warmth.

One day, while I was wandering around, I ran into an old classmate. He had been extremely poor during his school days. Though he was still poverty-stricken, he remained optimistic in every regard.

"Hi Kim!" he said. "Long time no see! How are you? Let's go to get a cup of coffee." His imposing manner overwhelmed me in a way it had not done before.

"You know," he continued, "I was an idealistic person during our school days, but I have now chosen reality in place of idealism. I no longer believe in any metaphysical dogmas or 'isms'. Those may save us after we die, but for now, reality is reality. Those doctrines are nothing but a vacuous drone of mindless mosquitoes. By dint of my friend who has a powerful background in the military government, I barely was saved from the gutter of cockroaches. Do you still trust in those illusionary words? I have not forgotten the friendship you showed me in our school days. It seems to me that you are now looking for a job, aren't you? Why don't I take you to where I work? Let me know what you decide. I'd like to help you. Don't think too much; rather, think simply. The truth is in the present, not in the future." He gave me a wink.

I realized that he had become a shrewd agent, finding disgruntled and displaced people who were unhappy with the military dictatorship.

"You sold your soul for a piece of bread," I muttered.

"Do you remember, Kim? I told you that my family completely collapsed during the Korean War. My father was a Communist who was shot to death after being arrested by the police. The ideology that my father worshiped destroyed my family. Day and night, we trembled under the watchful eyes of the police. Eventually, hunger and persecution drove apart my four brothers and three sisters. I am still angry that my father relegated his young children to the bleak wilderness for his own vain, ideological ambition. Do you think that ideology can be justified in the face of all the blood that has been sacrificed?" As he spoke, he waved his hands in agitation. I wondered how long this diatribe could last. I finally interrupted him.

"Well," I said, "my present plans are to go abroad. I have made up my mind to leave Korea."

After a short silence, he began to rain bitter reproaches on me. "Why? To escape? You coward! You are a traitor to the fatherland. We will never have a second Korean War!" He barked these words at me as if he were a dog gone mad.

Stunned at his abrupt and rude words, I responded with some of my own. "Fine, you go your way and I will go mine. Go ahead! Try to dig out a life in this land!"

We left each other quite awkwardly. As I walked alone down the street, I thought about his violent words. He thought it was a betrayal of the fatherland to leave, and that I would become a cowardly traitor. But, following this incident, the days rolled by and my father's dream of emigrating never came to fruition. I began to realize that I could not pin my hopes on some vague dream, and that I had to start living in the present, not in the possibility of the future. I began to look for a job in earnest.

One day I saw an advertisement for employment at a lumber company. I applied instantly for the job. During my last interview with the president of the company, he yelled at me, "Don't steal!" I got the feeling he was a snake, and I was a mouse in a hole. I was perplexed at his warning. What did he mean by that? I came to find out that he was closely linked with a high-ranking public figure. The president of my company was a kind of political pimp who could borrow as much money as he wanted from the banks, without a background check. This president and the politician seemed to gain maximum benefits from their relationship. They clearly leveraged their association to become the robbers of society.

The company was run with militant ruthlessness. If anybody complained, he was immediately either fired or relegated to a less important post. Both intimidation and appeasement were rampant in the office. The corruption of the senior staff was beyond description. When I tried to protest against their impropriety, they would come at me with a two-pronged approach:

"You don't know details of how this company runs. Do you understand what it costs to get things done? Don't be frivolous, okay? If you are not careful, things may get serious." When these threats didn't seem to work out, they then switched to another tactic:

"Mr. Kim, you are correct that what I am doing is wrong, but I am not the real villain here. Don't blame me. The real thief is our president. Do you follow me? Compared with him, I am nothing but a petty thief. I don't make enough money to feed my family. Mr. Kim, please look the other way, okay?"

What was said about the president of the company really shocked me. After that, I was torn about whether or not I should continue to work there. But, certainly, I decided not to argue with senior management anymore.

At about that time, my mother was busy with her matchmaking. Through her, I met a nurse who worked at the municipal hospital. She was good-looking, so I asked her out for a date. Everything went well. We enjoyed walking down the dusky road near a stone wall beside the Chang-Kyeung palace. The streetlights winked at us as if they were blessing our meeting. A faint thought knocked my mind that our encounter might be pre-destined; we might be made for each other.

"Miss Lee, I think I like you," I said, hoping for a positive reaction. I furtively glanced into her eyes to see if I could gauge her response. Her face looked stiff, but she showed no sign of disdain at my rude outburst. While we walked down the murky side road, she did not say a word. Without any plans for a future date, we awkwardly parted. I was not sure if she would contact me again. A day felt like a year.

One morning, an unfamiliar voice called my office at the lumber company.

"Hello," the woman said, "I am a friend of Miss Lee. If you don't mind, I would like to see you somewhere." That evening, Miss Lee appeared at the entrance to a coffee shop with her two friends.

"Oh, here you are. How are you?" asked Miss Lee.

"I'm okay. And you?" I stammered a little awkwardly.

Her two friends began to scrutinize me with their playful eyes. Their inquisitive stares made me feel even more nervous. I sat silently, smoking my cigarettes and drinking my coffee.

"Mr. Kim, relax. We are just Miss Lee's chaperones. We are not inspectors." They burst into laughter, as if they were watching a funny puppet show.

"It's cramped in here," Miss Lee said. "Why don't we go for a walk outside?"

Neon signs flickered as we enjoyed our stroll. The spring breeze gently blew her long, black hair. "Mr. Kim," she finally said, "If you don't mind, I would like to introduce you to my father tonight." I was surprised by her special invitation. I instantly accepted the unexpected proposal. We quickened our pace and headed for her home.

"Welcome! Please come in, young man," her father said in a strong northern accent as he greeted me with warmth. "I hear you are a native of the north. I, too, am a refugee who crossed the 38th parallel. It has been a long time since I left my parents and siblings. I am not sure if I will ever see my family again. I may die before the reunification of the country is realized. I understand you are a veteran of the Vietnam War. I, too, am a veteran, of the Korean War. I was wounded in the battle to retake Seoul, just after General MacArthur succeeded in the Inchon landing operation. A war fought between brothers is a tragedy. The memories of the Korean War fill me with a profound sorrow. I have counted every day since then as a bonus. I was lucky to escape with my life. Anyway, young man, I want you to know that I trust my daughter. If you like each other, I give you my blessing."

Six months after meeting her, we were married. My personal life was going smoothly. However, general political and public life was another story. The military regime ran the country with a tight fist under the "Renovation Laws." If you complained about the government, you were arrested without the need of a warrant. Freedom was extremely limited. Fear was rampant throughout the country. Father's assessment that the military regime was suffocating the public was correct.

In early of April 1974, my employer, the lumber company, was faced with a serious crisis. The president and all the senior staff members were simultaneously arrested by the police. There was a rumor that the politician who had supported the company had fled to another country, abandoning all his cronies. The afternoon of that same day, a black Jeep screeched to a halt in front of my office. Two stout, plain-clothed policemen rushed into my office. They smirked as they looked around; they acted as if they were looking for a criminal. "We are here from the national police headquarters." One of the policemen glared at me. "Where is your director?"

My boss, Mr. Lee, had already fled. "Let me tell you something," one policeman said. "We are going to stay here until you bring us your boss. Do I make myself clear?" I called around as if looking for my boss, but of course he had already gone. The two policemen flew into a rage. They got close to my face. "And just who on earth are you?" they asked in a menacing manner.

"I am just an acting director," I stammered.

One of the men flopped down into my chair and proceeded to rummage through my desk. One of the policemen was so upset that the veins in his neck were bulging out. He shook his finger at me and said: "Listen you! Tell your boss to come to the national police headquarters. Do you understand me?"

Rumors spread that the police were torturing the president and his staff members. It seemed to me that the company, and my job with it, was about to collapse. My wife and I concluded that we had no choice but to go abroad. My wife immediately applied for an immigration grant to America. The process dragged on. At long last, in the spring of 1975, we received an American immigration visa. I tendered a letter of resignation to my company. I was nervous and excited at the thought of starting over in an unknown world.

Before we left, I made a pilgrimage to my grandfather's self-exile, deep in the mountain valley. As a token of respect, and in accordance with Confucian courtesy, I bowed, knocking my forehead on the paper-covered floor before him. When I finished explaining my plan to emigrate to America, I was met at first with complete silence.

Grandfather finally broke the tension. "Listen carefully, my grandson," he said. "My time is running out. I was a successful man in the north. However, I lost everything when the country split in two. Your uncle was killed in the war and the fate of your aunts is unknown. In any given moment, everything can be reduced to ashes. Wherever you go, and whatever you do, remember to place more importance on your spiritual life than on making money. I would like to leave my collection of poems to you. They represent all the poems that 1 have composed throughout my life."

His speech was tender, and I was deeply touched. "Grandfather! I will always remember your words, and I will long treasure your legacy. These poetic works will be passed down from generation to generation." His face seemed to be fixed into a mask, trying to hide the bitter sorrow he had been forced to swallow.

A few days before I was to depart for America, I mailed a farewell letter to him. But to my great surprise, he came to Seoul to see me off personally. I never would have expected him to make such an arduous journey at his advanced age. He wanted me to go with him to the Lim-Jin pavilion that adjoined the 38th parallel. Our trip was characterized by cold and drizzling weather that plagued us on our way to the scene of our country's tragic division. When we arrived at the top of the pavilion, my grandfather fixed his gaze to the north, where a dense fog enveloped the greenish mountains. He seemed to lapse into his own world. The sad memories he contemplated at that moment were beyond sharing.

After a long pause, he pulled a piece of blank paper from his pocket and began to jot down a poem, using Chinese characters:

Mounting the top of Lim-Jin pavilion
to gaze at the homeland of the northern part.
The clouds and the mist which veil the mountains
and rivers, blind me.
Why did the division of this nation happen?
This is a terribly bitter and indignant thing.
Oh! what day will the reunification come?"

"Grandson," he finally said, "you keep this poem. It might be the last I am able to give you." His eyes were filled with tears and I sympathized with his melancholy mood. From the tone of his poem, I realized how much the division of the country had affected him. Of all the destructive vermin that had plagued the Korean peninsula in the past thousand years, the "division" might very well prove to have been the worst.

At that moment, a wedged squadron of wild geese was seen flying into the sky north of the 38th parallel, letting go a distant scream.

"Out! Out! The cursed 38th parallel!" I had a soundless scream inside me.

I went to say goodbye to my dear grandmother early in the morning before my departure for America. Disturbed by my news of leaving, she asked, "What did you say? Where on earth are you going? America? You are going to be a refugee again? When will you be back? That wicked 38th parallel! It is the fault of the 38th parallel!" She was speaking in a trembling voice, letting the shadow of sadness overtake her wrinkled face.

She must have realized that my journey to America would mean a permanent separation. Teardrops rolled down her wrinkled face and her mournful cry turned into a gushing release of all of her pain. My heart was torn. Her crying did not decrease; on the contrary, her wailing turned into a rippling river, and then transformed into a wild storm rich with the tone of despair. Her sad wail became a sorrowful song that permeated my mind. It occurred to me that her sad melody was her entire generation's melody, written with all the pain and suffering associated with life.

The Journey to the West

Filled equally with apprehension and hope, my wife and I boarded a plane for America. In plain words, this was a reckless venture. I had nothing to sustain us financially when we arrived in the U.S. The only thing I could count on was my own, small body. The huge metallic bird carrying us soared into the highest heavens. It reminded me of the mythical giant bird, Bung-Se, that the ancient Chinese philosopher, Chuang-Tzu, had fictionalized. We were gliding in balance over the white carpet of fluffy clouds. "Look out there," my wife exclaimed. "Isn't it beautiful?" A mass of mountain-shaped clouds sailed leisurely in the infinite opening between the heavens and the sea. However, I did not have the inclination to enjoy this time of leisure. I was too busy worrying about what was to come. My thoughts chased after each other like shadows in a dream. Eventually, I shut my eyes and indulged in a little rest.

"Wake up! This is America!" my wife said excitedly as she pulled on my sleeve. At last, the giant bird was touching down smoothly onto the ground at Los Angeles International airport. Feeling very out of place, I was only slightly reassured by the warm greeting we received from my wife's friend, Mrs. Chun, who had been in America for a year and had a small nest for herself and her husband in downtown Los Angeles. "Welcome, friends!" Mrs. Chun beamed. "Let's go to my apartment. You must be tired. You know, America really is an earthly paradise flowing with milk and honey!" Mrs. Chun spoke glowingly. Her enthusiasm was a bit overwhelming. The broad leaves of semitropical plants could be seen through the windows of the white van that Mrs. Chun drove. The plants seemed to be bobbing their heads in a welcoming manner, greeting the newcomers. "Did you know that the state of California alone can feed the world's population for more than seven years?" Mrs. Chun continued as though she were a spokesperson for the state of California.

Mrs. Chun lived in a small studio with her husband. The day after I arrived in America, I applied for a room nearby. Even though I did not yet have any income, I was quickly approved as a monthly tenant. My heart was overjoyed at having secured a dwelling. However, I soon became restless in my desire to obtain a job, as our meager funds were depleting. One morning, a tall, slender man knocked on my door and introduced himself to me: "My name is Kim, Ki-Jung. I have been in America for two weeks. In Korea, I was a pastor, but now I need to get a job here to survive. I plan to go job-hunting tomorrow. Would you like to go with me?" I replied quickly that I would, of course.

The next morning the pastor led me to a bleak field where oil was being drilled. "Look at those iron masses. Those machines are pumping 'black gold.' We might be lucky someday to find some gold of our own!" Mr. Kim stopped at one of the many warehouses that were scattered around the oil field. I tagged along at his heels. The company was operated by the Japanese.

"Hello, *Watakushi wa, Kitei Gin san desu*," he spoke in Japanese, as if he considered his former Japanese surname to be a great honor.

"Are you Japanese?" an Asian man asked in English.

Mr. Kim replied, "No sir, my name was *Kitei Gin* while Korea was under Japanese control. If you hire me, I will render you devoted service."

The pastor's words shocked me. "Shit," I grumbled to myself, "how disgusting! What servility!" Despite his earnest flattery, no job was offered.

On our first Sunday morning in America, Mr. Kim knocked on my door again. "Hello! Would you like to go to church?" he asked. I was curious, and instantly consented to his suggestion. The church was a one-story building that served as the pastor's private residence as well as a church. To distinguish it from the other houses in the neighborhood, a small, white wooden cross had been stuck onto the roof. Mr. Kim introduced me to the minister, Mr. Chang, who ran the private church. The Reverend Chang was a tall man with a stout frame. He looked as though he could be a tough army general. "Welcome, brother!" he said, holding out his large hand.

After the service, he held a barbeque in his backyard for all the church-members. "Mr. Kim," he said to me, "if you have any spare time today, I would like to talk with you. Feel free to come into my study after the party." I nodded in agreement, and shortly, found myself sitting face-to-face with Mr. Chang in his personal library. "Mr. Kim," he began, "relax. Don't be nervous. I understand your present state of mind. I know that you are stressed. However, I have no doubt that you will fully adapt to your new life in America. I know that you want to be successful here. If you don't mind, I would like to explain to you why I came here." He gulped a glass of water and continued, while I sat sipping tea, content to listen to his story.

"In the fall of 1961, several months after the military coup succeeded, I was called into the office of a general whom I had respected throughout my long military career. At the crucial time that the coup was carried out, I was a lieutenant colonel, acting as a special aide to the general. I prepared the notes for his speeches. He said to me, 'You have done a good job for me for a very long time. As you know, our new, revolutionary government needs professional men of all skill levels. I think you can best serve your country by going to America to study. After you have finished your studies, you may come home and I will support you in any way I can.' I trusted the general. I hoped that I would be the next secretary of foreign affairs.

"Before I left Korea, the general made certain that I had plenty of money to assist me. However, it took me a long time to figure out that the general and his cronies had conspired to purge the political landscape of certain men. At first, I was furious at being duped, but then I concluded that I should stay in America for the rest of my life. I am a refugee from the Communist north. I have nothing to return to. I have become a permanent stranger.

"One day, in an attempt to fill the emptiness of my life, I happened to skim through the Bible. While I was reading some of the scriptures, these words from the gospel according to St. John, caught my eye:

The spirit gives life, the flesh counts for nothing. Then you will know the truth, and the truth will set you free. Peace I leave with you; my peace I give you. I do not give to you as the world gives. Do not let your heart be troubled and do not be afraid.

These phrases made me believe that nobody could save my depressed soul except Jesus Christ. Mr. Kim, don't trust anything in this world. Don't look for paradise on earth. What we see with our mortal eyes is nothing but an apparition.

At that moment, I was drawn to a life with Jesus. I immediately changed my studies' major from political science to theology. This internal, spiritual revolution was totally different from the military coup I had participated in. I made up my mind to seek a life worthy of Heaven. I no longer have any animosity toward the general I worked for. On the contrary, I am a much happier man now. Mr. Kim, do not worry too much. God will guide you."

For all of his solace, his personal sermon didn't do much to alleviate my anxiety. Despite my continued efforts, I was unable to find a job. My wife was beginning to worry. It was time for another drastic change.

My wife urged me to go east. She had a friend who was established in Maryland. With nothing to keep us in Los Angeles, we again took flight like a wandering flock of birds. My wife's friend lived in a garden-like city, whose summer colors were now hiding under the autumn tints of red, yellow, and orange. We arrived in Maryland in the last days of October 1975. My wife and I took a walk one day to enjoy the fall colors. As we kicked at the crunchy leaves, my wife was full of hope: "Good luck will come to us here, won't it?"

Sharing her delightful mood, I was happy to chime in: "That's right. This is our last stop. This land will be our final haven. No more escaping. I'm going to die here." With the help of kind neighbors, I was easily able to get a job in a warehouse as a full-time employee, as well as a part-time job on the side. Though it was hard, my new life in America seemed to be on course.

In January of 1976, five months after I had left Korea, the sad news reached me that my grandmother had died. A photo sent to me showed her dead body thrown into a frozen hole in the ground. She had desperately yearned for her son's return, and to be reunited with the two daughters who had been trapped in North Korea. The thought of her heartache broke my own heart yet again. The memory of her wailing resounded in my soul. She had been the very picture of grief during the divided times. Her fervent hope had been that there would be a reunification of Korea and that she might see her children again. She had hoped and believed in it, as others believe in the Second Advent of Christ. She had died without receiving that closure. Nevertheless, her dream will never fade away.

Waving the White Flag

The same year that my grandmother died, my father was finally able to fulfill a dream of his own. He flew to South America with his family of six. But, after he had been there for some time, I received a letter from him. He was not able to make any foothold in South America. My heart sank. His dream must have been shattered. In June of 1981, my father made a sudden appearance in the Washington, DC area. He looked fatigued and dejected, as if he were waving a white flag. He was 62 years old.

"I had no choice but to come here," he told me. "I am tired. I cannot endure another odyssey." He spoke as if he had resigned himself to his fate. Though I was very surprised by his unannounced arrival, I was happy to comfort him.

"Don't worry, father," I replied. "Everything will work out. I will apply for your green card as soon as I can. In the meantime, relax."

During the same time, I'd found out that my grandfather in Korea was terminally ill. On the day my father actually became a permanent resident of the U.S., I phoned grandfather in Korea. "Grandfather!" I said. "Father will be there tomorrow!" I tried to soothe my grandfather over the telephone. My grandfather died a few weeks after my father went to see him in Korea.

Many images of my grandfather flashed before my eyes. I was sorry he had to lead such a tragic life. I remembered the sad poem he had written and given me on the Lim-Jin pavilion. My father said that he was glad he had been able to be at the deathbed, and that grandfather had had a bright look on his face, as if the gloomy past had been erased. My father seemed to be full of new spirit: "I would like to make a fresh start in America." For the first time in my life, I saw him smile like a child.

"Don't worry, father," I told him. "We will forget about the past. I think that America is our last haven. As far as I can tell, there is no absolute poverty, no terror from military dictatorships, no academic cliques, no chronic sectionalism, and no fear of war. America is the land of opportunity."

He agreed. "I cannot complain about my present situation. I hope you feel free from now on. I think that optimism is better than pessimism."

Somehow, my transition to American life went smoothly. I was able to open a gift shop in a historical Washington, DC district called Georgetown, which is situated along the Potomac River bordering Virginia. There are many European-style houses clustered between narrow roads that spread out like a spider's web. The area was flooded with waves of pedestrians of all sorts, at all times, as if it were a cultural exhibition center. But the most interesting event was the annual Halloween parade. Every year, people dressed in grotesque demon costumes would come in flocks. Halloween evening, the Georgetown district would be bustling with energy. The "dead spirits" from the grave were busily preparing themselves to "rise up" again, moaning, screaming, and laughing for the event. But, as midnight neared on that special night, the festival would reach its climax, and the streets would be filled with living "ghouls." Once each year, the living and the departed would join in reconciliation.

I really enjoyed watching the crowds of people streaming in front of my store. My business was doing well. I would have been happy to keep my store in Georgetown until I retired. However, circumstances beyond my control changed my plans. The building that housed my store was sold. But, I told myself, "where there is a will, there is a way." I was lucky enough to find an empty space in a different district of DC, called Dupont Circle. The building owner was kind enough to accept my application for the lease without the usual red tape. I leased the space on the spot.

Dupont Circle was different from Georgetown in several ways. Dupont Circle was home to many fine art galleries, and to many gay people. I was shocked to see so many gay people, strutting on the streets in a fashionable way. This was something I had never witnessed in my mother country. Every once in a while, they would have a large-scale parade, as if Dupont Circle was their holy Mecca.

One day, a doctor stopped into my shop with a black-and-white photo of the famous Japanese novelist, Mishma-Yukio. "I need this framed," he told me very politely. But he continued to bring in the same photo of Mishma-Yukio, to be framed, every other week. I was curious why he needed so many of the same photo. One afternoon, the doctor came in again with the photo of Mishma-Yukio. "Mr. Kim," he said. "Please take this picture. This one is for you." He looked me in the eye and spoke very amiably. Though I was perplexed by his gift, I received it innocently. He smiled at me and said, "Mr. Kim, any time you want to, come and visit my house, okay?"

With another odd smile on his face, he gave me his business card. Then, he stopped coming to my shop. After a good long while, I realized that his gift had been a meaningful invitation. "You missed a wonderful chance to be with a wealthy, gay partner," my wife would tease me, while giggling. Men holding men's hands; women holding women's hands: this was to be seen all over the Dupont Circle area. At first the extraordinary sight of intimacy between them was confusing to me, but, little by little, I developed a feeling of goodwill toward them, because they were of gentle humanity.

It seemed to me that everything was progressing without a hitch. Father would lend me a helping hand with odd jobs. He seemed to be delighted and continued to keep a look of boyish simplicity on his face.

A Song of Farewell

As the proverb states that light is always followed by shadow, my father's roadmap to the new American life was plagued with an unseen obstacle. He was urgently admitted to the hospital with thrombosis. After his operation, he was never quite the same as before. He became tired quickly, and he had a haze about his eyes. His blank expression grieved me. I longed for that sharp look that used to intimidate me in my youth.

One morning, my father called me. His voice was very low. He wanted me to drive him to his doctor's office. By the time I reached my father's residence, he was almost unconscious and was swinging his arms in the air. With a trembling hand I called 911. The ambulance arrived quickly. They drained his lungs, which were filling up with water. This emergency measure saved his life.

The doctor at the hospital said that my father's kidney function had completely failed. Once he awakened from unconsciousness, my father gave me an awkward smile. "I think my time has come. I no longer have the power to go on." He was not happy about having to go to the dialysis center three times a week for the rest of his life. "I feel dizzy all the time," he said. "This is torture. Is there no way out?" Each day he complained more and more bitterly about his situation. He was aware that his life was coming to an end, "You know, son," he said, "my time is running out. Looking back, I think that my life has been a failure. I have never reached the promised land in this life. I have wandered from refuge to refuge ever since I escaped from North Korea in 1948. As my time is drawing near, I have come to realize that I could never find a place to escape to in this lifetime. The war will never cease and the sorrow will deepen more and more. I have no desire to go to the heavenly kingdom, as faithful believers should. I just hope that my body and soul will return to the mystery of nature. My only regret is to leave this life before the reunification of the fatherland is achieved. I hope that the day will come in your generation's lifetime. Son, do you know the witticism spoken by the ancient philosopher, Mencius?

Man lives in agony and dies in comfort.

"Now I am ready to go. When my eyes close for the last time, please have my body burned to ashes. I would like the ashes to be blown off by the wind over the Pacific Ocean, in the direction of my native land of North Korea."

Complicating matters, the doctors found another problem with father's vascular system. The doctor heartlessly explained to me, "One of his arterial tubes has bubbled. Without an operation, it could burst at any time. I know he is old and tired. It is up to him, whether he wants to go through the operation or not." But apparently, my father was not as ready to leave this world as he had let on.

"Don't worry, son," he told me, "schedule the operation as soon as possible." He urged me as if he wanted to end his painful life in haste. Consequently, as my father wished, I phoned the doctor to arrange the operation.

"This is one tough guy," the surgeon, Dr. Matthew, muttered as he examined father before re-admitting him to the hospital. The evening before his operation, I sat with my father as he had, what turned out to be, his last meal. A deathly silence hovered oppressively between us. I was compelled to say something.

"Father," I said, "you are not a failure. You have been a wonderful father." Another long spell of silence followed. Finally, he broke his reticence, pulling the white hospital blanket to his face to conceal his tears.

He said, "Son, you may go home now. I need to sleep." A ray of golden sunlight played across his lonesome bed.

The next morning, a man appeared in the waiting room and introduced himself to me. "I am the anesthetist. Don't worry; I will let him sleep well." After this remark, my father was wheeled away on his gurney through a maze of hospital corridors. After four or five hours of waiting, the doctor returned to hand us the news:

"He passed away."

Dr. Matthew delivered these three short words to me and quickly left. The word of father's death left me paralyzed. The unique bridge that had linked me to my father for more than fifty years had now been torn down. He lay on a cold, stainless steel table, looking like a stone Buddha. His complexion had turned yellow. His face and hands had become nearly frozen. Had his life been worth enduring, with all the hardships, only to come to this miserable end?

I reflected, and grieved, and decided that he was finally freed from all of his sufferings .But suddenly, I was reminded of a passage from Shakespeare that father liked to quote:

> *Life is but a walking shadow: a poor player that struts and frets his hour upon the stage and then is heard no more. It is a tale told by an idiot, full of sound and fury, signifying nothing. (MacBeth V/V)*

Passing on to the next life, he might find his ultimate haven, unattainable on earth. He might have been born as the eternal outsider who could never be compatible with the harsh realities of the world. With the passage of time, my grandparents had closed their lives with deep regret, and my father left this world in bitterness.

I will be the next to go. I am living in the twilight of my life. Every time I think about each of my personal hardships, I shudder in distress. All is eventually doomed to ashes. Moreover, the hope of unification that my grandfather desired, many years ago, has gone unfulfilled. I now have to pass on this message of "unification" to the fourth generation: my children. When will the vicious, vermin-infested "division" be stamped out? When will it all be over? I walked out of the ICU where my father lay "sleeping" like a statue on a narrow, steel table.

The cremation that he had desired fell through, due to the different opinions among his immediate family members. The day he was buried, I kneeled down beside his fresh, earthen snow-covered mound. I bid him farewell, and my warm tears fell on his frozen grave. I spoke to him. "Father," I said, "I miss you so much. Please rise again when your beloved homeland is reunified."

A high wind was wailing.

ISBN 142510021-X

9 781425 100216

Made in the USA
Middletown, DE
18 September 2021